THE LOCH EWE MYSTERY

BILL KIRTON

For the many friends with whom I sailed on Loch Ewe.

CHAPTER ONE – TWO WORLDS

Ben wanted to fight the air. Not with guns and blasters and all the things the characters used on his friend Charlie's X-Box, but with thinking and dodging and, well, just beating it. He was standing at the school gate, waiting for Charlie, and the air was icy and sliding between his scarf and coat to dribble its fingers in a cold line across his neck. He pulled his scarf tighter, which worked for about two seconds, then decided that magic was the only answer. He thought about his various words and chose the second on the list, Boxylog. He took a deep breath, said 'Boxylog' very loudly and spun round on one leg. Right away, his neck felt warm and there was no wind on it. He knew it was because his spin had taken him round the end of the school wall, where there was more shelter, but he preferred to believe it was thanks to Boxylog.

He thought everything was magic. That slice of air that he'd just beaten had come looking for his neck from the snows in Finland, Norway or Sweden. It nosed and sniffed its way across the North Sea, past oil platforms and over fishing boats, thinking to itself all the time, 'I've got to find the gap between Ben's coat and scarf'. He wouldn't say anything to Charlie about the magic. Charlie didn't believe in that sort of thing. He thought everything could be explained, everything made sense, and he always had numbers and figures to prove it.

As soon as he arrived, Charlie started talking, as usual. He didn't seem to notice the wind that grabbed his words as soon as they were uttered and flung them inland towards other towns where they'd be whipped into the gaps between other scarves and coats. Ben had a vision of clouds of Charlie's sentences tumbling across Scotland, scraping across people's cheeks, bouncing off buildings. scouring hillsides and eventually hurtling across the Atlantic and on into America. But then, why should they stop there? They'd go on, lifted into other winds, handed on across continents and other oceans, and that meant that one day they'd probably be back. Ben smiled to think that next week or the week after, he and Charlie might be walking along this same street while the words that Charlie was now saying would come rushing past them, sunburned from a spell in the tropics or deep frozen by their contact with the Arctic seas.

'What's funny about that?' asked Charlie.

'What?' said Ben when he realised that Charlie was actually expecting an answer.

'Why're you smiling at that? I don't think it's funny. He was in hospital for a week.'

Ben had obviously missed a great chunk of Charlie's speech and was completely lost.

'Sorry. Didn't hear what you said properly. Must've been the wind.'

'Force six, strong breeze, winds 22 to 27 knots. Googled it this morning. Anyway, you can tell from the trees.'

'How?' asked Ben.

Instead of answering, Charlie took out his smart phone, did some quick thumbing and showed Ben the screen. On it was a list of numbers with some words beside them.

'See? Beaufort Scale, it's called,' said Charlie. 'All about winds.'

He pointed at the screen and read some of the words there.

'In a strong breeze the branches of large trees sway and telegraph wires hum.'

'I'd call this more than a strong breeze,' said Ben and immediately, Charlie was off again.

'No, that's the official things they say about it. Look at the chart, the different wind strengths …'

Whatever they talked about, Charlie had always read about it somewhere or seen it on the internet and was always eager to tell Ben about it. In lots of detail.

Ben listened as his friend listed the different things the wind did. It was still all full of numbers, but there were other things, too. Just like the wind that had scratched icily at his neck, the ones Charlie spoke about were strange, living things, which gave special mysterious signs to show who and what they were and tell you what they were going to do.

'So, when leaves and small twigs start moving about, that's a gentle breeze, and it's a force three, and flags start to move out from flagpoles.'

As Charlie talked, Ben imagined the start of the wind as it came creeping in, rustling a few leaves to begin with, making the smoke from chimneys drift, then warning people that it was really on its way by rattling their windows, and finally terrifying them by uprooting trees and throwing bricks and chimney pots about.

Charlie recited the signs for a force seven.

'Walking difficult. Whole trees move. Dust flies high.'

And Ben was on a harbour wall, scanning the trees inland, feeling the dust spin up, and bending into the air as he made up his mind to put to sea in the three-masted schooner that lunged at its anchor out in the bay.

'Where are you going?' asked Charlie, breaking the spell that was beginning to grow in Ben's mind.

'Jamaica and the China Seas,' said Ben, before he realised that Charlie had put his phone away and was asking about something else.

'Really?' said Charlie, his eyes wide and his face shoved forward in amazement.

Ben tried to remember the last thing that Charlie had said.

'Sorry, what did you ask about?' he said.

'Your holidays, of course. Where are you going for them?' said Charlie, a little sharply. 'What's up with you? You going deaf?'

'No, of course not. It's this force seven.'

'Six,' insisted Charlie. 'Well, where are you going?'

'I think it's called Aultbea,' said Ben.

Charlie stopped and looked at him. Ben was forced to stop as well and half-turn to look back at his friend.

'Where's that?' asked Charlie, genuinely puzzled and interested.

'Somewhere on the West coast, I think,' said Ben, turning again and continuing homewards.

Charlie scuttled to walk beside him.

'West coast of where?' he asked.

'Here,' said Ben, 'Scotland.'

'What? That's not a holiday.' said Charlie.

3

'Yes it is,' said Ben.

'Course it's not,' insisted Charlie, anxious to help his friend to understand and to start having a good time. 'It can't be if you're staying at home.'

'We're not. We're going to Aultbea. We're going to live in a croft.'

When he heard this, Charlie stopped again and made a strange noise.

'What?' said Ben.

'That's terrible,' said Charlie. 'Crofts are awful.'

'Why?' asked Ben.

'They're hovels,' said Charlie, confidently, remembering a TV programme he'd seen. 'Straw on the floors. No paths. Mud everywhere. No electricity. No television. Cows in the bedroom. Nothing but misery. You can't go and live in one of them.'

Ben didn't know enough about crofts to contradict his friend but he knew his mum and dad wouldn't take them to the sort of place that had cows in the bedroom. As usual, though, Charlie seemed pretty certain of what he was saying. Ben felt a little beat of anxiety that made him want to reassure himself as well as his friend.

'That's only what you've read,' he said. 'This croft we're going to is different.'

Charlie shook his head and started walking on again. Ben said a magic word to himself and had an idea.

'It's got a computer,' he said.

'It can't have,' said Charlie. 'How can you have a computer without electricity? Batteries don't last for ever.'

Ben was desperate. Yet again, Charlie seemed so certain. He always had the facts.

'This one's got a venerator,' he said.

'What's that?' said Charlie.

'For electricity,' said Ben.

'You mean a generator,' said Charlie.

'Yes,' said Ben. 'And electronics.'

Charlie's head was shaking more and more, and there was a sort of smile on his lips. He obviously didn't believe him. Ben needed to get away from facts. Time to get magic again.

'And it's got a tunnel,' he said. 'And sacred stones. And … and … Drebsigoes,' he said, picking the fourth word on his list.

Yet again, Charlie stopped. Ben was getting fed up with this stop-start walk.

'What's Drebsigoes?' asked Charlie.

'Ahah,' said Ben, turning and walking on again.

'You made it up, didn't you?' said Charlie.

'Maybe, maybe not,' said Ben.

'OK, what sort of sacred stones are they?' asked Charlie.

'What I said,' continued Ben. As usual, the minute he invented something, he began to believe in it. 'They're sacred stones. The Highlanders used to worship there hundreds of years ago. Sacrificed things. Used to take goats up there and ... boil them.

'Boil them?'

'Yes. It's a special place. Haunted, too.'

'And what's the tunnel for?' asked Charlie, who was obviously not convinced.

'Escapes,' said Ben, with growing confidence.

'Escapes from what?' asked Charlie. 'Boiling goats?'

'No. When a goat's boiled, it's boiled. It can't jump out of the pot and chase you.'

'It could if it was just lightly boiled,' said Charlie. 'Sort of simmered.'

'I'll find out all about things like that when I'm there,' said Ben. 'I'll be investigating mysteries.'

'Catching flu from living in a croft more like,' said Charlie.

'And,' Ben went on, bringing the idea of his holiday back towards the truth before Charlie thought of any more questions. 'Dad's getting a boat for us to use while we're there. A new one.'

That did the trick. It was too much for Charlie to cope with. The holiday on which he'd poured so much scorn when Ben had first mentioned it was suddenly beginning to look and sound quite exciting, like on X-box only real. He didn't want to give up, though.

'So you'll be investigating your boiled goats and haunted sacred stones by sailing a boat down a tunnel, will you?' he said.

'Course not,' said Ben. 'The boat's for the loch. There's an island in the middle of it. We'll need to get out and look around that for ...'

He hesitated. His father had told him about a new boat, and about the loch and the island, but he'd only just got away with the story about the tunnel and the stones, so he decided that he'd better not start any new inventions. He finished his sentence tamely, '… stone circles and things.'

Luckily. Charlie had once gone to see a stone circle on a school trip, so the holiday discussion was left aside as he started explaining the differences between standing and recumbent stones. Ben was relieved. He didn't think his description of the holiday croft would last very long if Charlie really got going on it.

Soon, they'd reached the corner of Cameron Place where Ben turned and Charlie went straight on. They said goodbye and Ben started running. The wind really was biting at him, and he was keen to get home and drink some hot chocolate. As he ran, his imagination still changed everything he passed into something else. He didn't really understand why Charlie and his other friends spent so much time looking at the tiny screens on their mobiles when there were so many other huge things around them. Flower beds in gardens were lids over holes in the earth's crust. The daffodils and tulips of February were coloured flames blowing around the top of the shafts, and hiding the black depths. Lamp-posts were the ribs of a metallic dinosaur which had become radioactive because it was buried so deep in the ground. Even the stones of the houses groaned as he passed them, remembering that they had once been part of greater blocks sleeping under mountains.

This was Ben's world. He loved to let his dreaming take him away from cars and buses and pavements into another world of organisms, creatures, lives beyond the neat and tidy enclosures of Charlie's lengths, weights, depths and measures. He soared along the pavement, slicing like a blade through the wind, faster than a spaceship, quieter than an owl. At his front door, he stopped and looked through the window into the room his father called his study. He had no idea why it was called that because his father never did any studying in there. As he looked, however, it wasn't the name of the room that bothered him. He saw that there was something strange about it. It wasn't one of his inventions. He wasn't imagining anything. What he was seeing was real. But it couldn't be. When he'd left for school that morning, the room had been normal. Now, it was completely bare. All the furniture had gone, the pictures from the walls, the carpets, the curtains, everything. Ben opened the door with a funny feeling inside him.

CHAPTER TWO – THE EMPTY ROOM

He looked around carefully as he went in. Everything in the hall seemed normal. As he put his coat, scarf and bag into the cupboard under the stairs, he could hear his mother singing in the kitchen. He went in and she turned her head to look at him. He was surprised at what he saw. Despite the singing, her eyes were red and there were damp bits on her cheeks. She'd obviously been crying. But she smiled, asked him the same sorts of questions she always asked, told him there were some new biscuits in the tin and carried on working at something in the sink as if nothing were the matter.

All thoughts of hot chocolate had gone for the moment. His mother's tears and the empty room needed explaining. His mind, as usual, began to invent answers, but they weren't about magic because this was serious and real. Why would the furniture be taken away? Because they had to sell it. No, there were plenty of other things they'd sell first. And, anyway, who would buy an old desk and some chairs? What else then? So that the room could be redecorated? No, why should that make his mother cry? It must be something bad. He'd heard about things like dry rot and, although he wasn't sure what it was, it didn't sound nice and he could imagine tiny, furry, black gremlins chewing away inside the walls, turning them into powder so that they started to crumble and made the whole house come crashing down.

Was that it, then? The room had dry rot and the house was going to crumble away bit by bit. His bedroom upstairs was right over the study. He saw the study walls dribbling away into dry sand, a big hole appearing in the house beside the front door, and his bed hanging out over the space where the study had been. Then his bedroom fell onto the rubble, the hall collapsed, along with the kitchen, and eventually, where their house had been was just a heap of brick dust and powdered wood. His face was pale as he contemplated the disaster.

'What's the matter, Ben?' asked his mother, sniffing back another tear. 'You look ill.'

'Dry rot, I suppose,' said Ben, expecting her to confirm all his suspicions and tell him that they would have to move house.

'What?' she asked. turning to him in surprise.

'Not me. The study, I mean,' said Ben. 'It's got dry rot, has it?'

'Good grief, I hope not,' she said with a little laugh. 'Whatever made you say that?'

'It's empty. All the furniture's gone. And the carpets and things.'

His mother smiled again, and the expression on her face, despite the tears that were still obvious in her eyes, seemed genuinely happy. This didn't make sense. Straight questions and answers were needed. Ben looked into his mother's face.

'What's the matter, Mum?'

'Nothing. What do you mean?'

'Why is the study empty? And why are you crying?'

The questions made her laugh out loud, and for a moment Ben was afraid that she was mad or hysterical, like the women he saw sometimes in black and white films on television. He hoped she wasn't because the cure for that always seemed to be to slap the mad person's face and he didn't think he could do that to his mother.

Luckily he didn't have to. As she laughed, she showed him the reason for her tears. In the sink in front of her were four large onions which she'd been peeling ready to make soup. Ben felt very relieved as well as a bit silly for not having noticed them before. But there was still the empty study to explain. He asked her again why the room was bare, but she just gave him another smile and said, 'Ahah'.

She liked mysteries as much as he did and had often invented the wildest explanations for things Ben had asked about when he was little. When he was a toddler and lost a tooth, for example, she didn't just tell him about the tooth fairy; there was the tooth lorry, tooth librarian and tooth carpenter as well. And, when she told him stories, Cinderella's pumpkin didn't turn into an ordinary coach; it was a glass coach, with crystal wheels, cushions made of chocolate and a hollow roof filled with lemonade that Cinderella could suck through a golden straw as it drove along. Oh, and the horses always had jet engines in their heels and the shoe that Cinderella left at the ball wasn't a glass slipper, it was a glass Wellington boot.

Although 'Ahah.' was an answer he himself often gave, especially to Charlie, it didn't satisfy him and he was still curious about the bare room. He realised that it was all he was going to get for the moment, though, and he was at least glad that there was nothing wrong.

He took the milk from the fridge and poured it into a saucepan to make his chocolate. When it was ready, he carried it through to the study. The room looked strange, bigger somehow, and completely different from when his father's desk had been in it. Stranger still, though. was the effect the emptiness had on noises. His footsteps sounded flatter, his voice echoed and lingered as he tried one or two words, and even when he whispered, the hiss of his breath seemed to get bigger and run around the walls. It wasn't the sort of echo you get in caves, where your voice goes away from you and hangs high up in the air somewhere; it was a much closer echo which seemed to gather nearby.

Ben tried different noises from different angles: close to a wall, down in a corner, looking up, looking down. Each gave a slightly different effect. He concentrated on filling the room with layers of sound, getting rid of the emptiness by wrapping ropes of voice together and folding them in the air. As usual, he became so involved in what he was doing that he didn't notice his father's car arrive, didn't see the unloading of boxes from it, didn't hear the bumps and footsteps in the hall, and was taken by surprise when the study door opened and his father's voice, made tinny by the emptiness, said, 'Right, Ben. Work to do'.

Ben went out into the hallway where some of the boxes and things from the car had been stacked. There were two containers like tubs or buckets, two large thick polythene bags with metal and wooden things in them and two smaller packages. Still in the car there was one very big flat cardboard box. His father was already outside lifting one end of it.

'Come on then, get the other end,' he said.

Ben ran out, grabbed the box and lifted. It wasn't very heavy, but it would have been awkward for his father to manage it on his own.

'What is it?' asked Ben when they had carried it into the study and leaned it against the wall opposite the window.

'Ahah,' said his father.

'Yes, that's what Mum said,' said Ben. knowing that he would obviously have to wait to find out what all this was about.

They carried everything through and stacked it neatly beside the big box. When it was finished, they turned out the light, went out of the study, shut the door, and nothing more was said about it. His father went upstairs to wash and change, his mother talked to him about school, and everyone behaved as if there were no empty room and no mysterious packages.

Eventually it was time to eat, and Ben knew that both his parents were enjoying the curiosity which chewed away at his mind as they sat at the table. Every time he asked some innocent question which might give him some sort of clue. they laughed, said 'Ahah' again, or wagged a finger at him as if to say 'you won't find out that way'. In the end he gave up, knowing that if he tried not to be interested the time would pass much more quickly.

***

On the other side of Scotland, the wind was blowing even harder than it was outside Ben's house. Ewe Island was a huge dark humped shape lying out in the middle of the waters of Loch Ewe. The waves had built up under the wind and rolled in through the mouth of the loch to smash against the end of the island. The white spray of their crests blew high onto the cliffs that faced the Atlantic and everywhere on the surface of the water were the wild white horses set free by the force seven gale. Nobody watching them drive on up the loch would have understood why the French call them sheep; they had far too much power to be given such a gentle name. They thrashed and galloped and roared with the gale and, amongst them all, crouching black and still, was the island.

It lay opposite the shore of the loch along which spread the houses of Aultbea and Mellon Charles, but on a night like this, no-one was out of doors to look at it. In the darkness there was little to see, but on the North-West slope of the island's shoulder, the one which pointed towards Mellon Charles, something began which would only end when Ben came here. There was no-one there to begin it, no people were involved, no animals were there, but something moved.

***

Back on the East coast, Ben was still busy trying not to think about the boxes. In spite of himself, though, his mind kept moving back to them lying there in the dark among the whispers he'd left in the study. They were obviously things that had to be put together, built. But why in an empty room? Perhaps they were going to change the room into something else.

Maybe it was some sort of machine that made the room different. Maybe it projected pictures onto the walls so that you could change their colour by pushing a button. And, of course, once Ben had thought of that, his mind wandered into all sorts of possibilities. The wonderful machine changed not only colours, but textures. The walls became wood or paper, silk or stone; they changed shape so that sometimes the room was a cube and sometimes a globe. At one moment the study was a cinema as the machine projected television programmes onto a massive screen that was one of its walls, then with the press of another button, it folded itself up, sealed up the cracks under doors and around windows and half-filled the room with warm water so that you could swim around in the study-pool. There was nothing the machine couldn't do. Wait till he told Charlie about it; he wouldn't have read anything about that sort of thing.

He was just making the machine turn itself into a long tube which transported him up through the ceiling into his bedroom when his father's voice brought him back again.

'Right, we've teased you enough. Any idea what's in the boxes?'

'Some sort of machine?'

'Nope,' said his father. 'I'll give you a clue. Think of the summer.'

Ben's mind was blank. He thought of the summer. Warmth. That was all that occurred to him. Sun.

'Well?' asked his father.

'No idea,' said Ben.

'Forgotten our holiday already, have you?'

'No. I was telling Charlie about it on the way home from school. He says crofts are awful.'

As he spoke an idea came to him, and he said, 'Is that what's in the boxes, a kit for repairing crofts?'

His father laughed.

'No, of course not. Good old Charlie. No, this is a very comfortable croft. And it certainly doesn't need any repairing. But you're right about one thing; it is a kit. It's to build something.'

Ben thought again. One by one he went over the things that his father had said about the holiday when they had talked about it, ticking them off as he dried the dishes. At last he was left with only one possibility. But, surely, it couldn't be that.

'It's not a boat. is it?' he asked slowly.

'Yes,' said his father. 'That's it. It's our new boat. We're going to build it. You, me and mum. How about that?'

'Build it? Us? Where?' said a dubious Ben.

The answer did nothing to make him any less dubious.

'Here,' his father said. 'In the study.'

Ben didn't immediately share his father's obvious enthusiasm. The first time his dad had talked about a new boat, Ben had imagined a proper boat, one for fishing or sailing. But if they were going to build it themselves, in the study of all places, what sort of boat could it possibly be? It couldn't just be a model, not with the study cleared out like that. But it couldn't be a proper boat either. Could it?

His father noticed the quiet and the look on Ben's face.

'What's up?' he asked.

'Nothing,' said Ben. 'I was just wondering what sort of boat it was.'

'A dinghy,' came the reply, still enthusiastic. 'A dinghy you can sail or row or put an engine on. Don't you think we can do it?'

'It's not that,' said Ben, 'but it must be pretty small if we're going to build it in the study.'

His father shook his head.

'No, it's not small. In fact, one of the first things we've got to do is measure the study to make sure there's enough room. And then, even more important, we've got to measure the door to make sure that, when the boat's finished, we can get it out without knocking a wall down. Come on.'

In the study, the three of them measured the doors and unpacked the boxes. At last, Ben's father stopped and said 'There you are. Our boat'. Lying on the study floor were lots of flat bits of wood, two buckets of some gluey stuff, some bundles of copper wire, several packets of nails and pins and some plans. The three people who had unpacked it all were sitting in the middle of it looking at the photograph of a boat sailing smartly along, its hull gleaming white under a pair of red sails, and Ben was wondering how on earth they were going to transform the mess around them into such a beautiful object.

CHAPTER THREE – CHARLIE'S INVITATION

In the weeks that followed, every spare minute of Ben's time was spent in the study, carefully reading the plans and instructions and seeing, to his delight and surprise, a dinghy exactly like the one in the illustration gradually growing on its supports on the study floor. It really was amazingly easy to build it. So easy, in fact, that Ben secretly wondered whether it really would be just as good as the boats he'd seen raking back and forward across the water when they'd crossed the bridges over the Tay or the Forth.

When he told Charlie about it, Charlie was burning with curiosity. Eventually, one afternoon, he took pity on him and, as they reached the end of Cameron Place, he said, 'Why don't you come and see it?'

'Thought you'd never ask,' said Charlie and started hurrying ahead towards Ben's house so quickly that Ben had to run to catch up with him. When they got there, they said hello to Ben's mother, who liked Charlie and was pleased to see him, and then went straight into the study.

As soon as he saw the dinghy, Charlie said 'Wow' and reached his hand out to run it over its sides and along its gunwales, just saying 'Wow' over and over again.

Ben started to explain how they'd made the various bits, how they were joined, what was going to happen next and anything else that came into his excited mind. For a change it was he who was chattering away and Charlie who was listening. They walked round the boat, looked at all the seams, inside and out, knocked on the buoyancy tanks to hear the hollow sound, touched the seat, the mast step and the casing for the centre board, and Ben relived all the pleasure he'd already had in helping to make it.

Charlie couldn't possibly go home to a house which didn't have a dinghy in it, so they asked Ben's mother if he could stay for tea.

Charlie couldn't possibly go home to a house which didn't have a dinghy in it, so they asked Ben's mother if he could stay for tea. When she said that of course he could, Charlie phoned his own mother to tell her and went straight back into the study to wait for Ben's father to arrive so that work could start again. As they waited, they each took pieces of sandpaper and rubbed at the wood, which was already very smooth because Ben spent all his spare time sanding it down. Each time they rested, Charlie asked more questions about where the boat was going to be launched and where they'd do their sailing.

As his friend answered, he gradually became more and more greedy for information about Loch Ewe. Ben had been looking at books and maps and websites, and the names they'd given him were even richer than those in his list of magic words. His imagination grabbed them and expanded them and the picture he painted made Disneyland seem like a boring mudpatch. He told Charlie of mountains called Slioch and An Teallach, of Loch Torridon, Beinn Alliein and Sgurr Fiona and of the giant hollow scooped out of the side of Beinn Eiehe called Coire Mhic Fhearcair. He spoke of the picture he'd seen of Flowerdale Forest, which, in spite of its name, looked like the rocks of the moon. He used names like Greenstone point and Gruinard Bay and made them sound like places from Treasure Island. And both boys were thrilled at the thought of all those wonderful places waiting quietly on the West Coast for Ben to arrive and launch his boat amongst them.

***

As the boys dreamed their dreams, it was raining gently on Ewe Island. Amongst all the giants that Ben had been mentioning the island was only a rock. At its highest point it stuck just over two hundred feet out of the sea. But still, as the rain fell on its shoulders, the movement that had started back in February slowly continued. There were no men or sheep near the granite slab that stood looking towards Mellon Charles, but around it in the ground, the displacements had started. Things were changing. The earth was beginning to prepare unexpected pain and danger for the holidaymakers.

***

Charlie stayed the whole of that evening to help them, and he worked so hard and so eagerly that Ben's father was very impressed. Charlie was happy in his work and that meant that, after having had such a long rest as he listened to Ben, his tongue was ready to become very active once again. He talked about sailing, boats, winds and tides, types of wood, and poured out everything he'd been finding out about in the past few weeks. His talking didn't prevent him working and, each time a new job was found for him, he'd set about it cheerfully and with some new story or fact that he'd been reminded of. When they at last took him home in the car, he was very tired but was still talking about the big clippers that used to carry tea and grain around Cape Horn.

On the way home, Ben and his father laughed about Charlie's enthusiasm.

'He's always like that,' said Ben. 'Every time he sees or does something new.'

'Well, he certainly liked the boat. didn't he?' said his father. 'And he was a great help too. If he comes much more often, we'll soon be finished.'

'It's funny, really,' said Ben. 'When I first told him about our holiday he thought it sounded awful, but now I think he wishes he was coming with us.'

As they drove into the garage, Ben's father was quiet. He turned off the lights and the engine, locked the doors, and they both walked into the house and turned automatically into the study. They always did that nowadays. As they stood looking at their evening's work, Ben's father said quietly, 'He could come if you wanted him to, you know.'

'What?' said Ben.

'If Charlie wants to come and you want him to come there's room in the croft and Mum and I wouldn't mind.'

He paused to give Ben time to think about it.

'In fact,' his father went on, 'to tell you the truth, I was wondering whether you wouldn't get bored with just us there. What do you think?'

Ben didn't think he'd be bored at all, but he knew what his father meant. His mother loved painting and she'd be spending most of her time standing in front of her easel, and although he and his father would do lots of sailing, there were bound to be days when they couldn't and when his father would want to sit down with one of his books. Although he liked being on his own, he thought that his parents would probably give him a bit more freedom and worry less if they knew he was with Charlie.

'That'd be great,' he said.

'Right,' said his father. 'I'll ring his folks tomorrow evening and see what we can arrange. Come on, let's go and see what Mum's doing.'

They went out and closed the study door, leaving the boat balanced in the darkness.

That night Ben dreamed again of Loch Ewe and the mountains around it, but this time, instead of charting a solitary course across the white waves which crashed among the peaks, he stood at the deck-rail yelling orders to his lieutenant, Charlie, who fought hard to control the spinning ship's wheel. All along the shore, the shapes of the creatures who lived in the hills moved along with the boat's progress, waiting for the two friends to make a mistake, waiting to draw the boat onto the black teeth of the rocks.

In the middle of all the thrashing fury, Ben turned quickly to fling out his arm and point out a new direction to his helmsman. His hand banged against the head of the bed and he woke up and lay in the darkness. He had a strange feeling that he'd been woken by a noise coming from the room below. He listened hard but only the heavy silence pressed on his ears. He got up and went down to the study just to check that everything was alright.

The pale yellow light from the street-lamps washed into the room and settled on the edges of the dinghy, etching its outline against the night. Ben stood with his dream still echoing around in his head and before him in the room he saw only a ghost boat sailing slowly on the black air.

**

Five hundred miles south of Ben's house, in a small flat in north London, a man was making a telephone call to a hotel in Amsterdam. He was tall and broad with wispy hair and a dark beard with grey patches in it beneath his lower lip. He listened to the voice of the Dutchman he had phoned and grunted brief answers from time to time.

'Yes,' he said, 'Aultbea. It's on Loch Ewe. Between Gairloch and Ullapool.'

'Why d'you want to go there?' asked the Dutchman.

'Because that's where we've rented a place. It's miles out of the way. No-one will see us. We can keep the stuff out of sight until things are clear.'

'You realise how dangerous this stuff is,' said the Dutchman.

'Don't worry. It only needs a small boat and there won't be many people about at that time of year. The tourists don't come until later in the summer. There won't be any trouble.'

'That's what you say. How d'you know? How d'you know the police don't already know what we've got. They might be setting a trap in this Aultbea place already. We never …'

The man in London swore loudly.

'Look,' he said, 'just do your job. I'm telling you, there's no problem. It's the perfect place. Even if anybody did come along, we could deal with them.'

'How?'

'You know how. And there's plenty of places to bury them there. They wouldn't be found for days, probably weeks. So stop worrying, and get the boat ready. I want the stuff delivered in Loch Ewe in the middle of May. We'll take it from there.'

The Dutchman said nothing more. He put the phone back and looked at the newspaper on the table in front of him. It was open at a page of adverts for boats. He had to buy one ready to take some cargo to Scotland. The cargo hadn't yet arrived but he was right; it was dangerous. If the police found out about it, they would all be in jail for a long time. But he knew that the man in London and his friends were even more dangerous. If he didn't do as they said, he'd probably be found floating in the harbour one night. They weren't the sort of people you argued with. He pitied anyone who got in their way in Aultbea.

***

The following evening, Ben's mother was putting the final touches to a still life she'd been painting. Ben, Charlie and her husband were in the study as usual. She'd phoned Charlie's parents that day to ask if he could come on holiday with them and they'd said yes, but Charlie didn't yet know. She loaded her brush with paint and began touching light strokes to the canvas on the easel in front of her. Just as she was about to trace the delicate edge of the fruit bowl, a screech from the study made her jump and, instead of a thin line of orange paint a big splodge appeared. She guessed the reason for the screech right away. It was Charlie.

'Yes, yes,' he shouted. 'Oh yes.'

She heard his footsteps as he ran out of the study. He crashed into the room she was in, his face red and his lips stretched into a wide smile.

'Oh, thanks, Mrs Campbell,' he said. 'I'll behave, honest. Thanks.'

And, before she had time to reply, he'd run back into the study again, yelling 'Yes, yes.'

She laughed and began to paint over the splodge. It was nice to know that Ben would have company in Aultbea in May.

CHAPTER FOUR – LOCH EWE

At the end of the short Easter holiday came the day they'd been both waiting for and dreading. During the holiday they'd painted the finished boat with three coats of a rich dark blue on the outside of the hull and three coats of hard shiny varnish on the inside. The mast and all the fittings had been sandpapered and varnished and, on a bright April day, it was time to lift the boat off its supports and manoeuvre it through the doorway, into the hall and then into the garden. As Ben's father gave the instructions about where Ben and Charlie should stand, how they should grip the boat, which way they were going to turn it and so on, the boat seemed to get bigger and bigger while the doorway shrank until it looked like a mouse hole.

Charlie was muttering things like, 'Two metres. Not much clearance. And the angle of the doorway looks too sharp. There's sixty-three degrees to the wall.' Ben was stroking the boat, trying to calm it down ready for its first trip out of the room.

With hardly any effort, the three of them lifted the dinghy and tilted it so that its side was pointing at the ceiling. Ben's father went first, backing out of the door and lifting the front end of the hull higher as he went. Ben and Charlie were terrified that they would drop their end and ruin all the work that had gone into it, so they clung on tighter than they needed to and shuffled very carefully towards the door.

'Come on,' said Ben's father. 'There's no need to go so slowly.'

'Turn it now, dear,' said Ben's mother and, before they even had time to realise it, Charlie and Ben and their end of the boat had been pulled by Ben's father's movements out of the study and into the hall. They knew that the front door was bigger than the one they'd just come through, so that meant that the boat was free. They began whooping and laughing with pleasure, and soon they were able to congratulate one another as they lowered their burden onto the lawn, stood back and admired the beautiful, shining thing that they had made out of some bits of plywood and some glue.

They brought out the mast and stepped it, hoisted the red sails, and Charlie and Ben were allowed to sit in it and imagine that they were already flying across the waters of Loch Ewe with the waves punching into the hull, the wind flattening their hair, and the sails as tight as the wings of the gulls that hung in the air behind them.

***

Another boat which would soon be heading for Loch Ewe was riding gently on the water in a Dutch harbour. It was a small motor launch which had no mast or sails. It had a galley and a cabin with bunks as well as some space under the decking in the stern where food, water or cargo could be stored. The boat rode low in the water at present because the cargo spaces were all full of bits of rubbish, old ropes, cans, pieces of wood, and even stones. The man who had bought it was sitting in it, taking various measurements, and making notes in a small book. Before May, he had to get rid of all the rubbish, clean out the compartments and work out a way of making even more space available for cargo. He already knew how much room he would need. In the cellar of a smart house he had rented not far from the dockside lay heaps of packages bound up in waterproof orange wrapping. They had been delivered at three o'clock in the morning by two men who had brought them all the way from Turkey. The man knew that the packages were well concealed, but he was still anxious to get the boat ready and loaded and to set out for Scotland. He didn't have to be there until the middle of May, but he didn't like the idea of the Dutch police snooping around. He'd already seen enough of the inside of their prisons.

***

Once they knew that the dinghy wasn't going to stay imprisoned in the study, the relief that the four Scottish boat-builders felt was soon replaced by impatience. It was ready, it could easily be carried, and yet it still had to sit there on its supports in the study, miles from the nearest stretch of water. The evenings seemed long now that the job was over and Charlie especially was eager for the next stage of the process. He was fed up with just reading about sailing and not being able to do it so he switched his attention to the place that they would be visiting.

He read the terrible tales of the hardships of the Highlanders two hundred years before. They were miserable stories of families who were forced to leave their crofts because the men who owned them could make more money by having sheep on their land instead of people. And Charlie's statistics listed how many had died on bleak passages across the Atlantic to Nova Scotia and how many others had perished fighting their fellow Scots to protect lands belonging to people who never even came to see them.

Ben hadn't used any of the words from his magic list lately. Being busy with the boat was part of the reason but, also, he'd found plenty of magic in just thinking about sailing it amongst the mountains. Like Charlie, he'd read about the Highlands in one of his books, but it wasn't the numbers and dates that interested him, it was what they all meant. Charlie saw patterns, saw the people vanishing and the sheep multiplying. Ben, though, felt what had happened and, in his imagination, lived the pain of the scenes that Charlie was describing. Together they would build up pictures of the land as it was all those years ago, the people without money and often without food and with only a strange pride that kept them clinging fiercely to the small plots of land that their families had always farmed.

'The owners' men burned their houses. you know,' said Charlie, 'to make sure they didn't try to come back. Sometimes they burned them before the people left. Once there was an old lady in bed ill in one of them, and the man in charge told them to burn the croft anyway because she'd lived long enough and it was time for her to die. They set fire to the timbers of the house while she was still in bed. When she struggled out her blankets were on fire.'

Ben saw the flames, heard the cries of men and animals as the thick smoke blew across the heather, saw the broken families limping out of green glens towards hard, stony fingers of land pushed out into the sea. He found it hard to believe that it had all happened to let the tide of sheep flood up from the south to take their places.

At last the day came when all these imaginings were to be turned into reality, the Saturday morning in May when they started the drive across to Aultbea. Ben was disappointed to see that the weather was dull but his father said, 'Don't worry, Ben. If the weather's bad in the East. it means it'll be fine in the West. We always have the opposite to whatever they're getting over there.'

The car was soon packed and all that was left was the boat itself. Once again, they lifted it carefully round the various corners, out of the front door and, more easily than Ben would have imagined possible, they hoisted it upside down onto the car's special roof rack where in no time at all it was tied into place, with the mast lashed along one side of it. Ben didn't like to see it upside down like that. It didn't look right. It looked like some sort of lid that didn't fit the car properly. Charlie didn't like it either, but for different reasons.

'I suppose you realise,' he said to Ben, 'that it's ruined the aerodynamic efficiency of the car. There's a thing called a drag factor, which is a sort of equation between …'

'You're a drag factor,' said Ben. But he grinned as Charlie ignored him and, constantly thumbing through different screens on his mobile, carried on with his lecture. There were some things that never changed.

'If we average fifty miles an hour,' said Charlie, 'it should take us four hours forty-seven minutes.'

'Ah,' said Ben's mother, who was driving. 'I was planning on fifty-three point seven six miles an hour. What difference will that make?'

'Hang on, I'll work it out,' said Charlie, so excited and eager that he didn't realise she was joking.

Ben's mother and father laughed, Charlie concentrated on his phone's screen, and Ben settled back in the comfortable seat, his head buzzing with happiness and excitement.

His father's weather prediction turned out to be accurate. For the first half of their journey, the clouds stayed with them, but then, as they drove down towards Inverness and the beautiful Kessock Bridge, they saw the edges of the clouds begin to break up. In the direction they were heading there were just thin strips and little lumps of cloud, but mostly the sky was a shining blue, and underneath it lay the hills and mountains of Ross-shire. At first as they drove into them, Ben felt a slight disappointment. The countryside was a bit tame and didn't match the pictures he'd drawn in his mind of the haunts of the wild Highlanders. There were fields and farms and, although the snow still lay folded in the tops of some of the distant hills, everything seemed very civilised and not a bit historical.

It was only after they'd passed a fork in the road which offered a choice between Achnasheen and Ullapool that the country began to resemble the places he'd seen in his imaginings. They had chosen the Ullapool way and, in a very short time, the mountains suddenly seemed to have grown steeper and began to crowd in onto the road. There were fewer trees around, except for the great chunks of specially-planted dark green conifers that seemed to look out of place among the golds, greys and gentle greens that blended all the other parts of the land together. The stretches of water they passed weren't like the sort you see on postcards, but instead had the look of frosted glass, dark blue, dark grey and quivering under a raw breeze. And eventually, when all that surrounded them was tussocky grass, reeds, heather and granite, Ben knew that they had come to the country of crofts and the Clearances.

Everywhere, the descendants of those sheep that had driven the Highlanders away were wandering, singly or in clumps, up the hillsides, along the edges of the road, and even on the road itself. There was little sign of any other life. Here and there, small grey houses sat in protected corners, but more obvious to Ben were the ruins of little old cottages which had been abandoned many years ago, perhaps even at the time when the sheep had come.

As they drove on, they all seemed to be affected by the size and the emptiness of what they saw around them. Not only Ben and Charlie, but Ben' s parents, too, were quiet as they looked at the scarred hillsides, the granite shoulders of the mountains, the folds of heather and broom and the occasional rush of peat-brown water as it came out of the earth to find its way into the rivers that hurried along beside and under the road. In fact, the only thing that seemed at all modern or familiar was the road, which was fast and good, so it was rather surprising at one point when Ben's father said, 'You know what this road's called? The Road of Desolation.'

'Why?' asked Ben.

'The country, I suppose' said his father. 'It's pretty bleak. isn't it? And think what it must be like in winter. You see these poles along the road?'

The boys looked. At intervals, long poles stuck up out of the heather. Each one was red and white and looked like some sort of measuring stick.

'They show where the road is when the snow's covered everything up,' Ben's father went on.

'Must get pretty deep,' said Ben.

'Nearly two metres,' said Charlie, confidently.

'There you are then,' said Ben's father, turning round to look out of the windscreen again, 'the road of desolation. Two metres of snow seems pretty desolate to me.'

He pointed in the direction they were heading.

'See that?' he said. 'An Teallach. That's the name of that range. It's supposed to look like a man lying down.'

Ben looked. The range had several peaks and they were all high. He could see no man lying there, but he could certainly believe that a country like this was inhabited by strange figures, the creatures of myth and legend. These hills talked, the mountains turned to one another and moved slowly under their skins of gorse, pushing their long limbs out into the sea and remembering the men and women who had sheltered in the glens beneath them. It was even more impressive than his dreams had made it.

'Mistoria,' he whispered to himself, choosing a word from his list that wasn't quite right but which was the closest he could come to what he was feeling.

***

Only a very few miles in front of them, the granite slab on Ewe island was like the centre of a magnet which was pulling together the different pieces of the story. The movement in the earth beneath it had slowed but there were still little tumblings and slippings as the stone dragged them towards it. Their car was being drawn along the twisting Road of Desolation under the heads of An Teallach and Sail Mhor. At the same time, to the South West of them, the motor launch from Holland was sucked towards the point called Rubha Reidh. When it reached it, it would turn east and then south to sail into the mouth of Loch Ewe. The sun shone on the granite slab.

***

They drove up a track to their own croft in the middle of the afternoon. When the car engine stopped and they all got out, the first thing they noticed was the peace. There were no car noises, no people shouting or music playing. Instead, a light swish of breeze sifted through the grasses beside the track. Ben left the others as soon as he got out of the car and walked round the back of the cottage, looking at its walls, hearing the whispers of the people who had lived there down the years. He felt the stones of the little house growing out of the earth, knew that they had protected the Highlanders inside them from the winds of well over a hundred winters. He stood against the back wall and reached both his hands out beside him, pressing his arms hard against the granite blocks.

'I'm here,' he whispered, and he felt the stones settle.

The others shouted for him to come and help and, within twenty minutes, they'd unpacked the car and carried everything into the cottage. By the time they'd chosen their rooms, made the beds, stacked everything in cupboards and had some supper, it was well into the evening and obviously far too late to take the boat down to the water. Instead, they went for a walk to the edge of the loch to look for the best launching spots.

'There must be a beach,' said Charlie. 'There was that other white beach we drove past, just around the corner.'

'In Gruinard Bay you mean?' said Ben's father.

'Yes,' said Charlie. 'That can't be the only beach around here. Sand like that comes from erosion. Debris from the hills gets washed down into …'

Ben's father began snoring loudly and deliberately. But Ben felt a little shiver at the mention of Gruinard Bay. It, too, had an island lying just offshore. It looked inviting, the perfect place to take their shining blue boat. But, as they drove past it, Ben's father had told them that the whole island was once infected with a disease called anthrax, which killed animals and people alike. It used to have big notices, all along its shore, warning people not to set foot on the soil there. But the worst thing about the whole story was that the disease had been put on the island deliberately. Years and years ago, when there was a war, scientists had wanted to experiment with germs, and poor, lovely Gruinard Island had been chosen as the place for the tests. Ben found it hard to understand how anyone could come to such a place, look at its loveliness, and then deliberately infect it with evil.

His mood didn't stay sombre for long, though. Charlie was right; there were lots of white beaches and they soon found one which was well protected and almost totally free of stones. A path wide enough for the boat led down to it from the road and their smiles made it obvious that they'd found what they were looking for.

It was such a calm, quiet evening that they decided to climb a little way up the hill behind their cottage. It was quite late, but there was only a hint of copper-coloured darkness in the sky. They were used to such long light evenings over on the east coast where they lived, but here in the Highlands it was somehow different. The light seemed to belong to the air and hang on it like soft crystal. In the middle of the loch a small boat towed the great vee of its wake in from the sea towards the end of the island.

'That's where we'll be tomorrow' said Ben's father, pointing at it.

They all watched as the boat moved down the channel on their side of the loch.

CHAPTER FIVE – THE LAUNCH

The man from Amsterdam was glad to be at the end of his trip. As he tied his boat to the buoy beneath the slopes of the island, what he wanted most of all was to drop the orange packages he was carrying into the waters of Loch Ewe and get back home quickly. He waited until the night was dark enough to conceal him from any possible watchers on the shore, then he tied the packages to special floats and dropped them overboard. They disappeared immediately, but the floats kept them hanging in the water just a few feet below the surface. The floats were all knotted along a thin rope. The man tied the end of it to the mooring cable under the buoy and, as the tide surged, the packages were carried out in a line to hang unseen in the loch, waiting for the men from London who were going to collect them. High above, near the top of Ewe Island, the slipping movement that had started in February continued.

***

The next day was perfect for the launch ceremony. Ben had gone through his whole list of magic names but, in the end, decided just to call the dinghy 'Boat'. They lifted it off the car, took it to the beach, stepped its mast, got the sails ready and then eased it, stern first, into the water. It wasn't quite afloat because its bows were still resting on the sand. Ben's mother stood in front of it and pulled the ring on top of a can of lemonade. As it began to fizz out she held it over the bows and began pouring it onto the varnished gunwale.

'I name this boat Boat,' she said. 'May God bless her and all who sail in her.'

As the last of the liquid dripped from the can, Ben's father gave a final push. Boat floated free and bobbed just off the beach at the end of her bow rope. She pranced, skipped and settled on the little waves that ran to the beach and suddenly seemed to have lost all her weight and become a lively part of the surface of the loch.

Ben's mother didn't want to go sailing. She was here to paint. Now that the ceremony was over she was very keen to get back to the cottage, set up her easel, and start organising her things. She kissed her husband, said 'Have a good trip' to them all, and walked back across the sand.

It was the beginning of an exciting couple of days. Ben's father was a good sailor and teacher. Soon, the boys could take Boat out on their own and get her swishing across the surface, spinning through the wind from tack to tack and looking as if they'd spent their whole lives on Loch Ewe. Charlie preferred crewing to being at the tiller. It gave him more time to comment on how the sails and centre board worked together, explain why reaching was the fastest point of sailing and lecture them on what things were called, how they worked and where they came from. Ben smiled and laughed as he chattered on, feeling all the time the rhythms of the Highlands, the breeze on his face and every little heel and pitch which Boat made under him. He felt her grab at the parcels of wind that darkened the surface of the water and quicken her pace as they arrived.

Charlie enjoyed Ben's reactions, too, feeling them colour his own explanations. He'd quickly found that he couldn't get a signal on his phone. Ben's dad wasn't surprised. He told him that there were still lots of places where reception was poor, especially in remoter areas such as this. It just meant that, for a change, Charlie was living fully in the world instead of seeing it on a screen. And he and Ben really were a team. Together they learned to understand how the character of the wind changed as it made contact with Boat, tumbled off her sails and created a tangled mass of air behind her as she skipped through it. The value of every experience they had was doubled as they approached and described it from their different points of view. It was like having two holidays in one. And most of all, it was like belonging to a place, feeling as if they were a part of the air and of everything else around them.

On the second evening, Ben's mother was in a specially good mood. That afternoon, she had been working on a particularly difficult bit of the seascape she was painting and seemed quite pleased with the result. The canvas was on her easel just inside the door. Just by looking at it Ben knew that his mother felt exactly the same way he did about this place. In the painting, the sea seemed to move towards the island and reach greenish fingers towards its rocks, creamy clouds lifted over the greys and browns of the mountains like warm breath, and she had even managed somehow to colour the air. Ben and his father studied it all carefully. His mother stood beside them.

'What's it supposed to be?' asked his father.

'Piccadilly Circus,' she replied seriously.

'Not many buses,' said Ben's father.

'I'll put them in later,' said his wife.

And they went to prepare the supper.

Ben knew that his mum and dad weren't like those of his friends. They were always playing tricks on one another, and his dad had a habit of singing very loudly when they walked along crowded streets, just to embarrass him. Once, in the park, Ben had run away from him and hidden behind a fence because his father had stopped at a litter basket beside which two women with prams were sitting and begun to search through it, pretending to look for food. With parents like that, life was never boring but quite often embarrassing.

The supper smelled good but they decided to go for another little walk before eating. They climbed up the hill from which they'd looked across the loch on their first night and set out across the peninsula to the north. Although Aultbea was the nearest village, their house was in Mellon Charles and just across the neck of the peninsula was another Mellon, a small hill called Meallan Udrigill.

At the top of the rise, they were all surprised at the number of little lochans they could see. All over the headland there were patches of water, some of them joined by small burns. Even the ground on which they were walking was spongy and bubbles squeezed up beside each footstep as they moved on. They had just passed three big round rocks with patterns of grey and yellow lichen on them when Ben's father suddenly called for them to stop. They stood together, Ben's father with his arm round his wife, and Ben and Charlie both leaning against the biggest of the three rocks.

'Look at that,' said Ben's father, pointing at a dip in the ground which they were about to cross.

The boys looked and were unimpressed. There was a big, bowl-shaped rock, some more grassy hummocks like those they'd already passed and some clumps of reeds.

'What are we supposed to be looking at, Dad?' asked Ben.

'Danger,' said his father.

They looked again and were still bewildered. The hollow was even more green and gentle than the slope up which they had just climbed.

'What's dangerous, then?' asked Charlie, 'the grass?'

Both boys laughed. But Ben's father didn't.

'Yes. Well, what the grass is growing on, really,' he said. 'Watch.'

He picked up a. small rock.

'See the nice flat bit between those three big clumps of grass?' he went on, pointing at the spot he meant.

The boys looked and nodded. He swung his arm and lobbed the rock in a slow curve towards the place. It landed near the biggest hummock and the boys were amazed when, instead of rolling to a stop beside it, the rock disappeared with a soft, sucking splash to leave a wet brown smudge in the ground.

'Wow,' said Ben. 'What happened?'

'I'm not sure,' said his father. 'That rock might be just under the surface, or it might be very deep down already. Look at how green it is, greener than other places.'

The boys agreed.

'And look at the planks there,' he went on, pointing to a place near the edge of the hollow. 'When folks have put planks down to cross places, it means that the places are pretty nasty, and maybe pretty deep. And when they're as green as this, with clumps of reeds all over them, it's best not to risk it. It's all marsh. The vegetation builds up on top of it and everything looks fine, but I'd rather not take chances with them. Come on.'

And he set off, hand in hand with Ben's mother, towards the higher ground of Meallan Udrigill.

The discovery had subdued both boys and as they climbed, they were quiet. Separately, they were imagining the darkness lurking just under that deceptive green patch, the hands of the blind greedy creatures who lived in the liquid peat which flowed under the crust of vegetation on which they were placing their feet so trustingly. The land had just swallowed the rock.

Once again, Ben recognised that he was in a place where he didn't have to invent things. Here, everything fitted together in a harmony – yes that was the right word to use – a harmony. And the things he only dreamed about at home really were part of this world, lifting in the air around him, moving in the ground under his feet, surrounding him with a life that had nothing to do with towns or houses or television.

***

As they walked the last few metres to the top of Meallan Udrigill, three men in a grey van were driving up a rough track near the village of Laide. One of the men felt very uncomfortable because he was tall and broad and fed up with being cramped in the passenger seat. It was the man with the beard who had given the orders to the Dutchman back in February.

'Is this it?' asked the driver as they bumped up to a large cottage with small windows.

'Can you see anything else?' said the man with the beard.

The driver said nothing, but pulled the wheel round so that the van turned into the gap in the wall where a gate had once been.

'God, what a dump. Where'd you find this?' said the third man, whose voice was like gravel and who sounded as if he needed to cough.

'How many neighbours d'you notice?' said the bearded man. 'And how many police-stations? And how much rent are you paying? What d'you expect for nothing? The Ritz?'

They all got out of the van and looked around.

'Won't be here long enough to worry about it, I suppose,' said Gravel-voice.

'Better not be,' said the driver.

The bearded man seemed to lose his temper. He grabbed the front of the driver's jacket.

'Listen,' he said, his face very close to the other man's eyes. 'I've had enough of your moaning, right? This is one of the biggest pay-days you've ever had and all you can do is squeak. In a couple of days we get the boat, bring the stuff ashore, then we're back home. So keep your whining to yourself, OK?'

The driver pulled his jacket away from the other man's grasp, spat on the ground to show his anger, but didn't dare answer him back. Both he and Gravel-voice knew how dangerous the man with the beard was. His name was Lomax. They'd seen him fight in pubs and streets and they didn't want him to practise on them. Anyway, he was right; they only had to spend a few days together, get the orange packages and then drive back to London and share out lots of money. Nothing could be easier.

CHAPTER SIX – OUT ON THE LOCH

The trouble started at the beginning of their second week. Ben's father had decided that they were now experienced enough to sail all the way to Poolewe, a village at the head of the loch. He calculated that it would take them most of the morning to get there. Charlie consulted the chart of the loch, muttered a lot and wrote things on bits of paper and agreed with him. They took several bars of chocolate and two large bottles of orange juice for provisions, put extra jumpers in a waterproof bag in case they got cold, and Ben's mother said that she'd drive down to Poolewe at about one o'clock to meet them for lunch.

As they packed their provisions in the special compartment in Boat's bows, Ben felt as if they were off on a genuine voyage of exploration. So far they hadn't ventured any further than just off the jetty at Aultbea, but this was a real journey, with a destination, and for the first time Boat would be right out in the loch on open water. He looked at the sea rippling its muscles between the beach and Ewe Island, the snatches of blue sky between the ragged clouds, and he gently stroked Boat's gunwale, feeling her quiver as the morning wind strummed in her halyards.

They set out early with the wind steady on their starboard side so that it was easy to point the bows across it and keep bundling along. Charlie and Ben's father could relax completely, lie back in the boat and watch the steep shore of the loch slip slowly by.

After just over an hour, Ben's father suddenly pointed over the port bow.

'Look,' he said. 'See how dark the water is there?'

The boys looked. There did seem to be a large patch of darker grey water in the middle of the wide stretch through which they were passing.

'What is it?' asked Ben.

'I'm not sure,' replied his father. 'Could be lots of things. Wind, oil, just a current even, but maybe it's grilse.'

'What's grilse?' the boys said together.

'Baby salmon – or small fish of some sort. You get lots of them at this time of year. And where there's grilse, there's mackerel. Let's go over and see.'

Ben eased the bows over to port and headed straight for the darker water. As he did so, his father took a fishing line from the compartment in the bows and began to make sure that there were no tangles in it.

'Have we got any bait?' asked Charlie.

'You don't need any,' said Ben's father. 'Not with mackerel.'

'They just commit suicide, do they?' said Charlie.

'Sort of,' said Ben's father. 'They're so greedy, they grab at anything that might be food. They think the hook's a little silver fish, so they jump at it.'

As they got nearer to the darker water, it was more difficult to distinguish where it began, but Ben's father dropped the line over the stern and trailed it behind them. Nothing happened. Ben and Charlie looked doubtfully at one another. Then, after about five minutes of quiet attention, Ben's father said, 'Ah well,' and started to pull in the line.

He made sure that it didn't get tangled with the mainsheets as it came in over Boat's transom. Ben tried to keep concentrating on steering but was fascinated by the fact that the line was zigzagging rather wildly through the water. Charlie leaned over and forgot all about the foresheets. Then, with a trumpet-call of triumph, Ben's father lifted the line and swung it into the boat with not one, but two flashing mackerel slapping their powerful little bodies back and forth as they tried to free themselves from the hooks.

Ben's father took them off the line and put them in the bucket that was tied under the thwart.

'There you are, you see,' he said. 'Tonight's supper. Fresh mackerel. I told you they were greedy.'

'Can I have a go?' asked Charlie.

'Of course,' said Ben's father, but we don't want to catch too many. There's no point in doing it just for sport. It's too easy.'

Ben held his course for Poolewe as Charlie prepared the line and then eased it gently over the side. He was astonished to feel, almost immediately, a hard pull followed by a constant trembling on the line.

'Is this a bite?' he asked.

Ben's father felt the line.

'Better get it in and see,' he said.

Astonished, Charlie began hauling in the line which he'd only just let out. When he lifted the last bit of it on board, he couldn't believe what he saw. The line had four hooks on it altogether and on each one was a threshing fish.

'See what I mean?' said Ben's father as he put them with the others. 'It's too easy altogether. We're right in the middle of a shoal. We could get a boatful if we wanted to.'

Charlie secretly thought that the probability of four fish striking at the same time on one line was unlikely. He was sure that there must be a degree of skill involved. Ben's father had only caught two after all.

The wind had freshened and soon they were all sitting on the same side of the boat to keep it upright as it reached on towards Poolewe. They were now in the most open stretch of water in the whole loch and the wind built up bigger sets of waves than those they were used to in the trips they made from their beach to Aultbea jetty. Boat climbed through them, slammed her bows into the bigger ones, slicing the water aside and pressing on across the wind. The exhilaration of the fishing combined with the liveliness of Boat's movements to make them all feel that this, at last, was an adventure.

Soon, they were pulling Boat up onto the shore beside the small jetty at Poolewe. Their morning had left them excited, exhilarated and very hungry. The chocolate bars hadn't been touched, but they decided that they would save them for the return trip that afternoon and wait for the arrival of their car. They sat down on the jetty and looked at the river tumbling under the bridge.

***

Ben's mother was not far away, driving down past Inverewe Gardens. She was singing as she drove along and she paid no particular attention to the grey van going up the hill in the opposite direction. There was only one man in it. The driver had left Gravel-voice and Lomax in Poolewe. They had met up with the Dutchman and been given details of the mooring buoy and how the packages were attached to it. Lomax paid him his money. The Dutchman grabbed the bundle of notes and, without even a goodbye, went straight back to his boat and set out on the long trip home, glad to be away from the police, the customs men, and, most of all, Lomax.

The other three had managed to hire the boat that they needed so badly. It was a long brown fishing boat and Lomax and Gravel-voice were at this very moment on board it, getting it ready for the trip up to Aultbea. All of them wanted to be away with their prize, back to the cities in which they belonged, away from these hills and lochs. Tonight, they would get the floating orange packages and bring them ashore to start filling the grey van. With luck, their work would be finished in two nights.

***

Boat's crew had just noticed their lunch driving over the bridge. The noises they made to greet it caused some alarm amongst a group of nuns who were on their way to visit Inverewe Gardens. Ben's father stopped to apologise and to explain that the two boys had just been let out of prison. The nuns frowned, then smiled at them, and Ben and Charlie, after making what they thought were the right faces, started galloping up the slope.

Lunch took a long time. As they ate, Ben's father told them about Inverewe Gardens, which were just outside Poolewe. Even though they were right up in the north, the climate in this little corner of the loch was mild enough to allow all sorts of exotic plants to grow there. The garden slopes faced south and west and the man who started them had built a big wall to protect them from the worst winds. It was all helped by the Gulf Stream, about which Charlie, of course, knew quite a lot. As the others concentrated on their sandwiches, he spoke about plankton, jellyfish and cold and warm currents. Now and then, Ben and his parents made little snoring noises but Charlie didn't mind.

Not long after they'd finished eating, they were eager to be back on the water. Ben's mother took the mackerel with her in the car and, in no time at all, the boys and Ben's father were pushing out into Poolewe bay and turning the bows to head out towards Ewe Island. As soon as they were out in the clearer water, Ben sensed that

Boat was beginning to feel different. Her movements were more urgent, there were rapid little shocks of air against the sail and shudders of water against the hull. The loch was preparing to show him yet another side of its character. So far, it had been gentle and magical. This afternoon, its mood was changing, becoming wild and unforgiving. A snatch of bad temper had arrived from the Atlantic. It made the loch angry.

CHAPTER SEVEN – THE ISLAND

It was obvious to Ben that the afternoon wind was altogether stronger. Boat was jumping and lunging about more than she had been on the way down. The scraps of blue sky had been filled in with hurrying clouds and the water was not the playful surge it had been when they started, but a rougher, angrier texture which at times banged hard against Boat's bows and scattered itself in splashes of foam. Ben knew that their ride was going to be rough when his father said, 'I think I'd better take her, Ben. This looks like a nasty squall.'

Ben moved forward to sit beside Charlie as his father took the helm. Boat slapped and crunched her way forward, and gradually the noise and the movement increased.

'Better take in a couple of rolls, just to be safe' said Ben's father after a while.

They lowered the sail a little and rolled it around the boom to make it smaller, then tied up the halyard again. Ben's father pulled the tiller towards him so that Boat turned away from the wind, her sail filled again and she was once more off, slamming across the churning water. They all concentrated very hard on keeping her upright and helping her to fight her way forward against the tumbling air, the waves and the spray. In their nervousness, they talked much more than they had on the way down that morning.

'It's only a squall. It'll pass,' said Ben's father, and added, 'I bet you know how squalls form, don't you Charlie?'

'Low pressure,' said Charlie, glumly. 'Sea evaporates and condenses at higher levels, then …'

He went on, but without the usual gusto. He had never been sailing in this sort of wind before and the experience wasn't all that comfortable. Suddenly, statistics seemed a bit out of place.

'How long do they last?' asked Ben.

'Depends,' shouted his father over the wind. 'They usually die away as quickly as they arrived. It's quite normal over here.'

It was hard work now. They were all sitting on Boat's port side and leaning out quite a long way to keep her upright as the wind tried to blow her over to starboard. Charlie clung on tight to his foresheet, Ben dug his feet under the toe-straps so that he could lean out further, and Ben's father kept letting the mainsheet in and out and sawing the tiller back and forward as Boat leapt up and over the waves and dug down the other side of them.

At one point, Ben's father caught sight of a long brown fishing boat which was well off their starboard side, its engine pushing it down towards Aultbea. He thought of trying to hail it so that they could take down the sails and ask for a tow, but it was too far away and the wind was too loud. Even if it had been closer, though, the two men on board would have taken no notice of them. They knew nothing about the sea and its dangers. Their fishing boat was simply a means of getting at the orange packages and they cared little for anyone else's troubles.

The squall persisted. More lumps of cloud came bustling in from the ocean, bringing more wind in stronger gusts. Boat was battling hard and making good progress, but Ben's father was getting anxious. All three of them were wet through by now from the waves that crunched against the hull and came spinning up at them, and the self-balers they had fitted to Boat were only just managing to get rid of the water which kept coming over the side. He looked up at the sky again, saw no let-up, and shouted, 'Right, boys, time to visit Ewe Island. I think we'd be better going ashore there until this blows over.'

The boys looked through the spray at the island. It was straight ahead of them and certainly much closer than the shore of the loch. Beside it, the water looked flatter and there was obviously less wind because the island itself provided a shield against it. As they got nearer, they began to feel the benefits of its shelter and soon they could relax a little as Boat stopped leaping about quite so violently and seemed to put more of her energies into pushing forward towards the shore. Their relief showed in whistles, bits of laughter, and silly jokes about shipwrecks. Charlie was soon ready to give his opinion on squalls after all and Ben and his father had to listen to a talk on high pressure, low pressure and occluded fronts which he remembered from a TV programme. Ben looked back to where the rushing air and tumbling water were still charging up towards Poolewe and said a silent 'thank you' to the spirits of the loch whose fingers had helped to guide them between the worst waves and the strongest gusts.

Under the lee of the island they couldn't feel much wind at all and the water was very flat. They stayed close inshore, let the sails down and paddled their way round to get into the bay which was opposite their cottage. There, they pulled her ashore and sat beside her, glad to let the tension drain out of their bodies. They remembered the chocolate which they'd saved and were glad that they'd put it in a waterproof bag because everything in Boat had been soaked. As they stood eating it, Ben asked if they could have a walk around while they were on the island.

'Let's go and see if we can find the farmer,' said his father. 'We'll tell him why we're on his land.'

They soon reached the farmer's cottage, halfway up the south eastern slope, but there was no sign of life. They knocked and called, but only their own voices and the blustering of the wind came back to them.

'Well, we've tried, Dad,' said Ben. 'Can we look around now?'

'I suppose so,' said his father, 'but let's keep our eyes open for the farmer. I wouldn't like him to think that we're wandering about his property just as we please.'

The wind was still fierce, so they stayed on the sheltered side of the island's backbone as they made their way towards the highest part, eager to get there both to look for the farmer and to survey the loch from this new viewpoint.

Directly on their path, near the top of the ridge, stood the great granite slab. No-one had been near it since February, when the movements had started. No sheep or birds had wandered past or over it, nothing had been there to upset its balance, only the rain and the whirling air. It looked black against the clouds as they climbed towards it.

When they got to it, Charlie noticed a rounded stone which seemed to be jammed against its base. It was smooth and had a pearly, marbled effect. He bent to pick it up, but it was stuck hard against the big stone. Ben and his father smiled at his grunting efforts.

'Leverage, that's what it needs,' said Charlie.

He looked around and saw another, longer stone on the ground nearby. He picked it up, jammed its end under the round stone and began using it as a small lever. At last, after more grunting and some shouts of encouragement from the other two, there was a slight scraping noise and the round stone began to move.

Suddenly, Ben's father stepped forward.

'Be careful, Charlie. It's not a good idea to ...'

His words broke off suddenly and the next instant was filled with terrifying and dreadful activity.

Ben's father had intended to warn Charlie, but even as he was speaking, he thought he saw the slab move. He jumped to push Charlie away from it. Charlie fell back as the round stone came loose, but Ben's father couldn't stop and his arm hit the rock. The weight of his body gave the final push that was needed. As he banged against it and fell, the slab, in what seemed like slow motion, bowed towards Aultbea then crashed forward. It hit the ground with a dull cushioned thud which was immediately covered by a loud scream from Ben's father. He didn't have time to get out of the way. His left leg was trapped and from the sound he made and the angle at which he was lying, it was obvious that it was broken.

Ben and Charlie were frozen with fright. Neither of them had been hurt by the slab, but the sound of Ben's father's scream had filled them with the agony he must have felt as it hit him and for the moment, they couldn't move. Ben's father was silent now. Ben looked at him. His face was greyish white, his eyes were closed and he was breathing very heavily. He moaned, and his eyes opened again. Ben was very glad. Without his father's help, he had no idea what to do.

'Are you alright Dad?' he asked, uselessly, because he could see that his father was far from alright.

'Yes. Fine, Ben. I just thought I'd have a lie-down,' said his father, who, through his own pain, could see from the boys' expressions that they were terrified.

'What can we do?' asked Ben, again knowing what a silly question it was because there was nothing that they could do.

'Just lift this thing off me and we'll go home,' said his father. Even as he said it, though, his face twisted with more pain, his eyes closed, and he fainted again.

Ben and Charlie looked at one another, each hoping that the other would know what to do. Charlie fumbled in his pocket and took out his phone but he knew it was no use. There were still no bars on the screen. No signal.

'We can't phone,' he said. 'There's nothing we can do here ourselves. We've got to go and get help.'

'Where?' asked Ben, even though he knew that Charlie was right. 'The farmer's not on the island.'

They both knew that. It left only one place. Mellon Charles. Ben looked at it across the water. It seemed such a short distance from up here, but he knew that from where Boat lay on the beach it was over half a mile away through the tumbling wind and water. Charlie knew what he was thinking.

'It's the only thing to do,' he said quietly.

Another moan came from Ben's father, then his eyes opened again.

'Listen boys,' he said, his teeth clenched tightly together. 'You'll have to collect some wood. We'll make a fire. Somebody'll see it.'

Ben knew at once that that would take too long and probably not work anyway.

'Everything's soaking wet, Dad,' he said. 'We haven't got any matches. It would take ages, and anyway who would see it?'

'It's the only thing to do,' said his father.

'No' said Ben. 'I'm going to sail across to the cottage.'

His father reacted immediately to Ben's words, wanting to tell him not to do any such thing. But the move he made caused the pain to flash through him again and once again he lost consciousness.

'You'd better not wait,' said Charlie. 'He's going to get very cold here and I don't know what shock does, but I bet he's got that, too.'

'Yes,' said Ben.

The pain on his father's face had made up his mind for him. There was no alternative.

'You stay here with him,' he said. 'Keep him as warm as you can. I'll get help as soon as I can.'

The two friends looked at each other again.

'Good luck,' said Charlie.

'Yes,' said Ben, knowing he would need it. Charlie turned his attention to Ben's father. He lay down and tried to use his body to keep the wind off him. Ben, hardly knowing what he was doing, started running down the hill towards Boat and the crashing waters of Loch Ewe.

CHAPTER EIGHT – THE PACKAGES

Down on the beach it was much quieter than it had been up on the hill. Boat lay there, protected from the wind by the island, and the waves that lapped around her transom were gentle enough. Ben was not fooled by the stillness, though. He could see the surface of the water jumping some fifty metres offshore. The wind seemed full of knives and needles. The confidence he'd begun to feel during the week was being buried under a layer of fear. But he had no choice.

He'd already decided, as he was running down the hill, not to bother with the mainsail. Once he was out on the loch, the wind would be almost directly behind him as he headed for the beach near their cottage. That meant that it might be dangerous with the big mainsail up. He would go quite fast enough if he only raised the jib and Boat would be much easier to handle. As he hauled on the halyard, his heart was banging away in his chest, but he was determined and Boat felt strong and reliable. He made the halyard fast, tucked the mainsail and its yard and boom along the top of the thwarts, sorted out the rudder and centre board ready to drop them into place once he was afloat and pulled his lifejacket over his head. Then, with a last look across the loch, he gave Boat a shove and jumped on board. He sat tensely in the stern, the tiller in one hand and the foresheets in the other as Boat hobbled through the flatter water inshore towards the much lumpier sea between her and her destination.

'Nothing is impossible,' he said to himself. 'All it needs is concentration. I just have to sit here and let this wind blow me across. Boat'll look after me.'

***

Not far away, the long brown fishing boat had appeared on the loch once more. The two men on board had gone in to Aultbea to make sure that she hadn't sprung any leaks during the trip up from Poolewe. The squally weather had sent most people indoors, so while the engine was still warm, they decided that it was probably safe enough to go and check that the packages were where the Dutchman had said they would be. They had turned out of the lee of Aultbea jetty and headed for the bay in Ewe Island just as Boat was leaving the calmer waters and feeling the wind gusting astern of her.

***

Even though the fishing boat was headed straight for him, Ben saw nothing of it. Boat drove confidently forward, the waves rolling up from behind her and lifting her stern before letting it wallow back down again as they pushed by underneath her. Ben had to work hard to stop the water forcing the stern round and setting Boat broadside on to the continual rushing folds of water. He felt very small and lonely and the loch seemed as big as an ocean. His arms were already beginning to ache and the foresheets had rubbed the skin from the fingers of his left hand.

It was as he passed close to the big mooring buoy that he sensed a strange feeling. Boat had been moving in all directions as she pressed forward, but her progress had been quick enough. Suddenly she seemed to quiver in a different way, as if she were trying to shake something from her. She jumped forward, but her bows swung round and she settled heavily in the water. The wind still billowed in the sail but she was corkscrewing, shrugging from side to side, unable to get further away from the island. Ben's fear clutched at his throat again. He was doing everything he should. There was nothing wrong, so why was Boat splashing so helplessly as if she had been caught in some snare?

As this question came into his mind, Ben realised that that was exactly what it felt like. Boat had been caught. It was as if a hand had stretched up from the bottom of the loch and grabbed her hull, or some part of it, to play with her like a toy boat in a bath. Ben leaned carefully over the side and looked along the hull. Water foamed past it, splashing up and over the gunwales as Boat strained to free herself. Ben saw nothing. He moved to the other side and looked again. Still he saw nothing but the angry water. He was very frightened now and had no idea what to try next. He wondered what Charlie would do if he were with him. He certainly wouldn't be imagining giant hands under the water. Ben tried to think as his friend would. Boat was trapped. It was definitely held by something under the water. What could it be?' The only thing nearby was that black mooring buoy. Yes, the buoy. Mooring ropes. Of course. It was obvious.

'Thanks, Charlie,' said Ben, as he moved to the side nearer the buoy.

He realised that the most likely 'trap' to have caught Boat was something that was attached to the buoy, an old mooring rope maybe, or a lobster creel. He looked much harder into the water. Boat's movements were still just as frantic, but now that he knew the sort of thing he was looking for, Ben quickly saw what might be the problem. There was something orange banging back and forth just under Boat's hull. It was hidden most of the time, but occasionally, as Boat swung with a bigger wave, it jerked into view before disappearing again.

The Dutchman had miscalculated. In conditions like these, with a strong ebb tide running against the wind, the rope to which he'd tied the packages was stretched out tight and everything was much nearer the surface than it was supposed to be. Ben reached down into the water. Boat heeled over and the water soaked his arm right up to the shoulder. As she came up again, though, his hand felt some ropes. He grabbed them and tried to pull them into the boat. From the way the ropes tightened as he did so, it was obvious that some of them were caught on Boat's centre board. He tried to pull the board up, but it wouldn't come. The ropes were obviously wound around it. He would have to cut them.

Hanging on to the ropes with one hand, he reached forward and grabbed the knife which was stowed in the bow compartment. He put the ropes across the thwart and sawed frantically at them. The knife was sharp. It didn't take long. As the ropes parted, he could feel Boat's response immediately. She turned her stern towards the mooring buoy and with a movement like that of a horse bucking to remove an unwanted piece of equipment, she swept away from it and jumped once more amongst the waves.

Ben pulled the end of rope he still held into the boat. An orange package came with it. He dropped it under his seat, grabbed the foresheets and started once again to plough Boat across the grey turbulence towards Mellon Charles.

***

He didn't know that the men in the brown boat had seen everything. Gravel-voice had spotted the dinghy first of all.

'Hey,' he said to his partner, 'that boat's tied up to our buoy, isn't it?'

Lomax looked where he was pointing.

'Looks like it,' he said. 'What's his game? Get that engine going faster.'

'That's as fast as it'll go,' said Gravel-voice.

They were too far away to shout a warning or to do anything, and when they eventually saw Ben hauling something orange in over the side, they were furious.

'It's the stuff,' said Gravel-voice in disbelief. 'He's got the stuff.'

'I can see that,' shouted Lomax. 'Quick. After him. He can't get far.'

Gravel-voice swung the wheel over. The bows came reluctantly round to starboard and pointed down the loch. The fishing boat and its angry crew were in pursuit and their thoughts were ugly.

They would have been even angrier if they'd known that one of the ropes which Ben had cut was the main mooring rope. Apart from the one package which Ben had pulled on board, all the rest were now on their way, in a tangled knot, towards the open sea. The tide, which had helped Boat on its way to Poolewe that morning, had now turned and was ebbing out of the loch, taking anything that floated with it.

***

Ben was still working hard to get Boat to her beach. Another squall of rain had swept in on the wind and the grey curtains it hung from the clouds kept the fishing boat invisible to him way off on his starboard side. He quickly regained the rhythm he had been learning before Boat was caught, and he knew now that they would make it. His fear was still burning in his veins, but he was thrilled to be crossing the loch and pushed forward by his anxiety about Charlie and his father, lying in the cold and soaking rain back on the island.

Boat surfed along with the waves in great surges as Ben heaved at the tiller. The fishing boat was much heavier and it rolled between the crests as its drumming engine pushed it sluggishly through the water. The race was very uneven. In what seemed like ages, but was in fact a fairly short time, Ben was coaxing Boat through the wide opening between the rocks into her own little beach. As he reached the sand, he let go of the foresheets and the sail was blown out to flap ahead of Boat as she drove her bows ashore. She was going too fast and Ben was thrown forward as she stopped dead. No harm was done, though, and he was able to jump out into the water, splash round to the bows and start pulling Boat up onto the sand. He tied the bow rope to a rock in case the tide came in far enough to refloat her, and ran up the track to their cottage.

His mother was inside reading. When he first burst in, she thought he was playing one of his jokes, but as he started to tell her the story, the tension he had been keeping inside him came rushing out. Along with the words came tears. They came so fast and so chokingly that he couldn't speak and for a moment he just clung to her, glad to feel her arms around him.

He got control of his voice again quickly, because he knew he had to, and through his sobs, told her about the accident. At once, his mother became efficient. Her pale face showed how anxious she was but her actions were quick. She went to Ben's room, brought clean, dry clothes down for him and told him to change right away. While he did so, she used the house phone to ring the police post in Aultbea. No-one answered so she had to leave a message. She grabbed other clothes and blankets from the bedrooms, put her own coat on, and before Ben had finished dressing, was bundling him into the car to drive to Aultbea for help.

When they got there, things were quickly taken out of their hands. There was no-one at the police post, but they went into the shop and explained the problem. The lady there phoned someone in the village and soon a fast boat was on its way across to the island. On board were several men, a stretcher, a complete first-aid outfit, some lifting gear from the local garage, and Ben and his mother.

They couldn't go into the beach on the island that Boat had used because the water there was too shallow for their boat, but there was a jetty a little further along the shore and once they had tied up alongside it, Ben began to lead them back up the ridge to where he had left the others.

When he saw them coming, Charlie waved, but as they arrived, just like Ben, he found that he couldn't say a word without bursting into tears. Ben gave him one of the blankets and said, 'That's what I did as soon as I got home.'

Charlie sniffed hugely and still couldn't answer him.

Ben's father was conscious, but he was shivering a lot and the rescue party were keen to get him back to Aultbea as quickly as possible. One of them gave him an injection which put him to sleep while some others rigged the lifting gear over the slab and slipped chains round it. One man pulled on one of the chains again and again. Soon the pulleys which he was working had raised the slab far enough to slide Ben's father clear of it. The injection was obviously powerful because there was no sign of distress from him as they tied his legs together and lifted him onto the stretcher ready to carry him down the slope. As Ben's mother began to follow with the two boys, there were tears in her eyes, but she made sure that neither Ben nor Charlie noticed them.

From that point on, both the boys began to feel very tired and very confused. Their work was over. They had been marvellous. Everybody kept telling them so. They had done all the right things, and Charlie's efforts to keep Ben's father warm had been as important as Ben's epic trip across the loch. Back in Aultbea, the doctor had arrived. He strapped up the broken leg and decided that the best idea would be to take Ben's father to hospital in Inverness. This left Ben's mother undecided as to what they should do. The lady from the shop who had phoned for help solved the problem.

'Well, you must go to Inverness with your man,' she said.

'But the boys ...' began Ben's mother.

'Don't you worry about them,' said the lady, in her soft Highland accent. 'I've had three of my own so I know fine what to do. And from the look of them, they'll not be getting up to any mischief for a while.'

She was right. While Ben's mother went off to Inverness with her husband, Ben and Charlie were taken to the lady's house where they had hot chocolate, biscuits and some special cakes which she had baked herself and which tasted like a combination of all the best things they had ever eaten. By the time Ben's mother got back it was nearly midnight and they were deeply asleep in a big double bed in a room at the very top of the house. The lady from the shop had thought of everything. She knew that the boys shouldn't be woken up and she had also realised that Ben's mother wouldn't feel in the mood to drive hack to their cottage on her own. Before she could think of protesting, the lady took her into a single room at the back of the house and insisted that it was hers for the night.

'But I can't stay here. You've already done so much. The ...'

'Goodnight,' said the lady with a smile, and she went out, closing the door behind her.

Ben's mother was as weary as the boys had been and she silently thanked the lady for her kindness and for knowing exactly what to do. Within ten minutes she was as deeply asleep as the two heroes in the room upstairs.

CHAPTER NINE – VISITORS

The next morning was even more like a dream than the previous day had been. The three of them sat in the kitchen having breakfast. The scene they could see through the window made it seem that during the night they had been whisked away to another place. The grey and purple clouds had disappeared, the surface of the loch, which yesterday had looked like heaving lead, was now a gently shifting blue carpet on which someone had sprinkled glitter dust, and in place of the tearing wind, they heard only the big stillness that came breathing out of the hills. Ewe Island lay peacefully out in its accustomed place, green and harmless.

Ben's mother told them what had happened in Inverness. Ben's father's leg was indeed broken but luckily it was only a simple fracture. It had been put into plaster and the doctors had decided to keep him in the hospital for a few days. There was no question of him coming back to Mellon Charles to finish the holiday, but equally there was no point in the three of them cutting short their stay.

As they tucked into some toast and jam, Ben's mother said, 'By the way Ben, Dad says he thinks it's probably OK for you to take Boat out on your own. Provided there's no wind, it's a flat calm and you don't put the sails up.'

The grin on her face made Ben realise that it was a joke. He thought about Boat and realised that, for the moment, he wasn't too keen to get back out onto the loch, even this morning, while it was looking like a crinkly blue mirror.

His mother had another, more serious message, too.

'Dad also asked me to say thanks,' she said. 'He says he'll thank you properly himself in time, but he wanted you to know right away that he appreciates what you two did for him and that he's proud of both of you.'

'All part of the job,' mumbled Charlie, who was easily embarrassed.

Ben just looked at his mother and winked.

When they were at last ready to go back to their cottage, Ben's mother tried to pay the shop-lady for her hospitality. With great dignity and kindness, the lady refused to take anything, saying that she'd been proud to help such fine young lads after what they'd done. Ben's mother secretly made up her mind that when she got back to Aberdeen she would find a present to send the lady to say thank you.

The drive back was relaxing. The sun was shining and Ben and Charlie couldn't help remarking again and again on how different the loch looked.

'A baby could sail across it today,' said Ben.

'A baby sailed across it yesterday,' replied Charlie, ducking as Ben threw a blanket at him.

'Well, I'm sorry that conditions aren't right for sailing,' said Ben's mother when Charlie had untangled himself, 'but they're fine for painting, and that's exactly what I'm going to do as soon as we arrive. So you'd better start making plans which don't include me.'

Soon she was turning up the track that led to their cottage. As they approached it, however, she stared hard through the windscreen.

'We did lock the door when we left last night, didn't we Ben?' she said.

'I'm not sure,' said Ben, 'I don't remember.'

Perhaps they had been in so much of a hurry that they'd forgotten. Yes, that must be the reason. Why else should the door be wide open as it was now? She stopped the car, they all got out and went into the cottage.

They knew immediately that the door hadn't been left open by accident. They'd had visitors. Angry, violent visitors by the look of the rooms. Drawers and cupboards were open and things were spread over the floor in knotted heaps. They couldn't believe it. This only happened on television. Ben's mother was white with the shock.

'Oh no,' she said quietly. 'Not burglars. Not here.'

Ben knew what she meant. To have thieves invade your home was terrible at any time. He had read about how the victims felt disgusted at the thought of other people touching their personal belongings, moving about amongst their private things. But this wasn't the same feeling at all. This wasn't even their own house. What did feel so wrong was that it should happen over here, amongst these lovely hills and lochs, where all the usual nastiness of living, the fighting and vandalism, the theft and destruction seemed an even greater insult than they were elsewhere.

After the first shock had passed, they looked through the rest of the cottage. Every room was in the same state. The intruders had looked everywhere. Clothes, books, dishes, clocks, radios, everything was piled together in sprawling heaps. Nothing had been overlooked. In Ben's mother's room, though, they made a surprising discovery. Right on top of one of the piles was a small glass box. It was the one in which she kept her rings, ear-rings and other bits of jewellery. The pieces it contained were not valuable, but the interesting thing was that they were all there. The thieves had obviously seen the box, handled it, but not bothered to take what was in it.

'What on earth did they take then?' said Ben's mother, puzzled at this discovery. 'There's nothing of any value at all here. These things were the only things worth taking. And the radio maybe.'

'But that's still here, too,' said Ben.

'I know,' said his mother. 'What were they after? It's a complete mystery. Surely they didn't come all this way just to tear the place apart.'

She had recovered from her shock and began to take control again.

'Well boys, it's no good guessing about the minds of the sort of people who do this,' she said. 'We'd better leave it all as it is. The police will probably want to see it. Try to find the kettle and some coffee. I'll ring the village.'

It took a long time for the police to arrive. They had a large area to cover and the local constable had been some sixteen miles away in Gairloch when they called. They inspected the damage, asked lots of questions, were astonished to hear that the victims of the break-in were the same people who had been involved in the previous day's rescue drama, and were generally mystified as to what was going on. They promised to do everything they could, but it was clear from the way they said it that they didn't think it would be much.

***

As the police drove away and turned left onto the Aultbea road, Gravel-voice was watching them through his binoculars. Lomax had left him there earlier that morning to wait for them to come back. The day before, their pursuit of Ben had been useless. By the time the two of them had reached the beach and found somewhere to anchor their own boat, Ben and his mother had left for the village. They suspected that whoever had sailed Boat to that beach lived in the cottage because it was so near. They forced the door and ransacked the place, eager to find out how many of the packages had been brought ashore. When they found nothing, their tempers were even worse than before. Gravel-voice had wanted to go and smash a hole in Boat's hull so that she couldn't be sailed again, but Lomax decided that it would be better not to do that just yet. Boat's owners might come back to use her to get more of their packages. If they did, he would be able to follow them and find out where they were hiding the stuff. At last, when it was obvious that no-one was going to return to the cottage that night, they drove back to their own place. Gravel-voice had come back early in the morning to keep watch while the two others went on to Aultbea to fill the fishing boat with fuel. The plan tonight was to inspect the moorings and find out just how much of their 'stuff' had been taken from them. After that they would decide what to do about the people in the cottage.

***

At the moment, these 'people in the cottage' were very busy. It's always much easier to make a mess than it is to clear it up and they were sorting out things that didn't belong together, refilling drawers and cupboards and generally trying to restore their home to the condition it was in when they had left it. It took them most of the afternoon and when the vacuum cleaner was switched off for the last time, they were tired and hungry. Charlie peeled the potatoes, Ben washed and sliced some mushrooms, and eventually, Ben's mother produced steaming plates carrying a mixture of mushrooms, bacon, smoked sausage, cream and herbs that smelled even better than it looked.

The three of them took their chairs and sat outside to eat it. The weather was warm, the food was delicious and at last, time seemed to be ready to slow down once more. Since their lunch in Poolewe, minutes, seconds and hours had crowded together, crushing and spilling forward and dragging Charlie and Ben with them on a wild race over which they had no control. Ben looked across at the beach on Ewe Island, took another mouthful of food, and felt everything settling back down into its rightful place.

It was obviously too late to do anything very adventurous and, anyway, they all felt that they'd had enough adventure to last them for several years. They ate some apple pie (which tasted very special because of the raisins and nutmeg that Ben's mother had added to it), talked a little, listened to the silence and began to forget the ugliness of the burglary.

Just past eight o'clock, Ben suddenly felt guilty that he hadn't been to look at Boat since their return. She'd brought him across the loch safely and he had just left her down on the beach and raced away. As he thought of the tangle in which he'd left the rigging and sails, he suddenly remembered the package that he'd pulled on board out by the buoy. In all the excitement, it had never been mentioned. In truth he'd forgotten all about it. After the gentleness of the evening, the memory of the package gave him a little thrill of anticipation. He was obviously recovering and ready for more surprises. He told Charlie and his mother about it. Their curiosity was immediately aroused and they decided that it would be nice to have a short walk down to the beach with him to say hello to Boat and to inspect her forgotten cargo.

Gravel-voice had been collected by his two companions much earlier in the afternoon, so there was no-one to see them as they turned down the track to the beach. When they caught sight of Boat, Ben's mother suddenly said, 'Oh, no Ben. Look.'

Ben was looking. He couldn't see anything wrong.

'What is it Mum?' he said.

'The burglars. They've been here too. Look at the mess they've made of poor Boat.'

Ben laughed.

'No, Mum. That was me. I'm sorry, but I was in so much of a rush yesterday that I just flung everything into her and hurried up to you.'

'Typical,' said Charlie.

They began to take the sails and rigging out of Boat to roll and coil them away. When everything was lying on the beach, Ben reached under the seat. There was nothing there. He leaned over and looked. Still nothing.

'Funny,' he said. 'It's not here.'

They looked amongst all the things they'd taken out and then had a thorough search of all the compartments where it might be hidden. The package had gone.

'It must have fallen out while you were crossing the loch,' said his mother. 'You said it was quite rough.'

'You probably imagined it all,' said Charlie. 'Your brain was crazed with fear.'

'I didn't imagine it and I don't think it fell over the side. It was under my seat, I'm sure of it,' insisted Ben.

'Well, it's not there now,' said his mother. 'Maybe the burglars came down here and stole it.'

'I wonder why,' said Ben. 'I wonder what was in it.'

'Long John Silver's treasure, I expect,' said Charlie as he started to roll the foresail into its bag. He had definitely had enough excitement for the time being and he was not sorry that the added complication of the mysterious package had disappeared.

***

He was right about it being treasure. The package was worth several thousand pounds to the three men. Every single one of the orange bundles was just as valuable, too. Ben's tangle with the mooring buoy had ruined their plans. They didn't know the other packages had floated away, though, and they were desperate to find them.. The one they'd taken from Boat was in a locked box in the back of their van. As Ben's mother and the two boys were stowing away Boat's gear, the men were sitting in a hotel in Aultbea.

They drank slowly from the glasses of beer on the table in front of them and said very little to one another. They were waiting for darkness to provide the cover they needed to go out to the mooring buoy and look for more of the orange packages. Nothing had gone right so far, and their bad moods increased with every hour they had to spend up here.

They left the hotel at eleven o'clock and were soon moored in the bay of the island. They switched off the engine and began their search. They looked all around the buoy, probing the black water with their boathook, but finding nothing. They got angrier and angrier. Finally, Gravel-voice did manage to hook a piece of rope. He pulled it greedily up over the side. The others leaned beside him but, instead of their precious packages, they saw only the cut end of the rope which had tethered them before Ben had run over it. Lomax swore and punched the metal cover of the engine. Gravel-voice spat into the loch and flung the rope back towards the buoy. All of their precious parcels had vanished. The cut rope was the final proof.

'You know who's got them, don't you?' snarled Lomax to no-one in particular. 'Them. Them over there.'

He jabbed a vicious finger into the darkness towards Boat and the cottage. Gravel-voice called Ben some very unpleasant names.

'Right,' said Lomax. 'They think they're clever. Think they've made a killing, do they? OK, we'll show them just what a killing really is.'

He had seen the boy pulling one of the packages on board his boat. So the boy must know where they were. He would either have to answer their questions or discover just how terrible their anger could be.

CHAPTER TEN – CAPTURE

The next day, the weather was still fine and Ben's mother was determined to get on with her painting. The boys weren't sure what they would do. They wanted something peaceful, something with no risks attached to it, a quiet, reflective day watching the grass grow. They sat for a while on the seat outside the front door. Ben's mother had already taken her easel and paints a little way up the hill behind their cottage to start on a new landscape. The morning felt warm and lazy. Eventually Ben said, 'We're not going sailing today, are we?'

'Not if you don't want to,' said Charlie.

'Do you?'

'No. Not really.'

'Right,' said Ben in the same sort of voice his mother used when she had made a decision. 'We'll just go and check that Boat's alright and maybe if the tide's low enough we can look for some sea urchins.'

'The tide won't be low enough,' said Charlie.

'How do you know?'

'It was coming in that morning we went to Poolewe. It'll be a week before it's low tide in the mornings again. Anyway, to get sea-urchins the tide has to be extra low. Spring tides, they're called.'

Ben stood up, walked a few paces, then turned and looked at his friend.

'D'you ever get fed up with being right all the time?' he asked.

'Never,' said Charlie.

The two boys were both aware that their friendship had changed since they'd arrived here. Ben was prepared to admit that he was impressed by Charlie's understanding of the differences between real wind and apparent wind when they were skimming along in Boat, and Charlie had often felt the shivers in his mind as Ben had talked about the beings that filled the hills around them. They were getting closer than they had ever been before.

When they got to the beach, Boat was waiting as patiently as ever just as they'd left her the previous evening. Her blue hull shone brightly and the sun's highlights were reflected in the varnish on her mast. They began re-tidying the gear once again.

***

All the time, they were being watched. The van-driver and Gravel-voice were back. They had driven Lomax to Aultbea. He was going to take the fishing-boat back to Poolewe. They didn't need it now that their packages had gone. If they had to go anywhere on the water, their plan was to use Boat to do so.

When he saw Ben unfold the mainsail and spread it on the beach, the driver became fidgety.

'They're going somewhere,' he said.

'Wait and see,' said Gravel-voice.

'Oh yeah. What if they sail off somewhere and don't come back?'

'Why would they do that?'

'I don't know. They've got the stuff, haven't they? No point in hanging around, is there?'

Gravel-voice looked at him with a shake of his head.

'You don't know what you're talking about,' he said. 'Look at them. They're kids, not villains.'

'Why're they packing the stuff away again then?' asked the driver.

Gravel-voice looked. The driver was right. But why would anyone unroll sails and then just roll them up again? There was only one answer. They must be getting ready to leave. He couldn't risk letting them get away while he was off fetching Lomax. He put the binoculars into their case and scrambled to his feet.

'Come on,' he said and began to climb down towards the beach.

***

Charlie and Ben were simply enjoying the warmth of the sun on their shoulders as they took lots of care to fold the red sails into neat parcels. They were so used to having the beach to themselves that the sight of the two men coming down the track towards them surprised them and made them feel a little uneasy. Charlie saw them first. He nudged Ben and the two boys stopped what they were doing and looked at them.

'Morning, boys,' said the bigger of the two men. His voice was strange, sort of low and scratchy. The sound was unpleasant. Instinctively, Ben didn't trust him. The two men stopped beside Boat.

'Nice,' said Gravel-voice, running his hand along her gunwale. 'Your boat?'

'Yes,' said Ben, warily.

The man walked right round Boat, looking at her all the time and nodding.

'Just the job for fetching things, eh?' he said.

Neither of the boys answered. They had no idea what he was talking about. He leaned over and picked up the mainsheets which were coiled neatly on the seat.

'Specially good for fetching things that don't belong to you,' he added.

There was distinct menace in his voice. After what had happened in the past couple of days, the boys could sense danger when it was around and this man sounded dangerous.

He continued to walk round Boat, swinging the mainsheets in his hand as he did so. The smaller man had said nothing yet. He'd been looking back up the track and around at the rocks. He too was nervous. Suddenly he spoke.

'Stop mucking about,' he said, almost in a whisper. 'Let's get on with it.'

'What's up?' said his partner. 'Afraid somebody'll come. Not a chance. Not round here. They can scream all they like. Nobody'll hear them,'

As they heard these words, Ben and Charlie knew that they were in trouble. The menace they had felt was real. Together, they turned to run back up the beach but even as the man had uttered his last words he'd begun to move. With two or three long strides, he caught and grabbed Ben and quickly threw the mainsheets around him, pinning his arms to his sides. As Ben tried once more to run, the man yanked at the trailing end of the mainsheet and Ben was pulled painfully off his feet to fall face down in the sand. The smaller man had grabbed Charlie in the same way and held him now while Gravel-voice got another rope from Boat to tie round him. Soon, the two friends were lying side by side on the sand. At first, they both screamed in their terror because they were sure that these men must be mad and intended to murder them. But, as Gravel-voice had said, there was no-one around to hear them. The nearest person was Ben's mother, and she was at this very moment up on the hill behind the cottage, humming to herself as she mixed another colour on her palette. Very faintly, in the distance, she could hear the boys' yells and she smiled to herself, glad that they were having a good time.

The yelling stopped as Gravel-voice leaned over the two boys. He picked up a handful of white sand.

'You're getting on my nerves,' he said. 'No-one's going to hear you. If you don't shut up, I'll fill your mouths with this.'

He meant it. Ben and Charlie had no choice. Their minds were blank with fear, but they knew that he had to be obeyed. The smaller man had been made even more nervous by the noise the boys had made.

'Come on,' he said. 'Let's get them away.'

Gravel-voice tugged at the ropes to drag them to their feet. They tried to resist, but that just made them fall over and the man continued to drag them painfully across the sand and pebbles. In the end, they had to submit to being pulled stumbling up the track towards the road.

In a lay-by just around the first bend stood the grey van. When they reached it, the driver opened the back door and Gravel-voice shoved the boys inside. The door was locked, the men got in the front and the van started off up the road. Ben and Charlie, already more terrified than they had ever been before, were clattered about the floor like sacks of rubbish, too scared to cry, feeling only the bruising of their bodies and the numbness of their minds.

When the van eventually stopped and the driver switched off the engine, they felt a massive relief at the silence. The door was opened, sunlight washed in on them, and they were dragged out onto the grass in front of the men's dilapidated cottage. Gravel-voice looked at his watch.

'No time for anything now,' he said. 'Lomax'll be waiting. You'd better get off and fetch him. I'll take care of them.'

Obediently, the driver got back into the van and reversed out of the gate onto the track. He drove off and the sound of the engine trailed away into the distance. Gravel-voice pushed open the front door of the cottage.

'In,' he said, jerking his thumb at it.

Meekly, because they had no option, the boys went into the dingy interior. It wasn't as light or as clean as their own cottage. As they looked around in the dimness, it was difficult to believe that outside, the morning was still bright and filled with sun. The man pushed them towards the stairs which led up to the bedrooms.

'Up there,' he said, and again they could do nothing but obey.

He took them to a room which had one small window, a wooden chair and a metal bed with no mattress or bedding.

'Here you are. Home,' he said, with a nasty smile.

Ben managed to speak.

'What for?' he said, his voice breaking. 'Why have you brought us here? You don't know us. Why are you doing this?'

'Oh, a speech,' said the man, pretending to look impressed. Then he jabbed his finger into Ben's chest.

'You'll find out everything you need to know soon enough, son. You'll stop playing the innocent. You'll remember the stuff you stole from us and you'll tell us where you've put it.'

'What stuff? We haven't stolen anything. Honest, I've no idea what you're talking about.'

'Oh?' said the man, pretending surprise. 'You didn't spend any time moored out on the loch the other day? You didn't cut any lines attached to a buoy? You didn't pick up an orange package? And I suppose we didn't find it under the seat of your boat when we looked. Try again son.'

'But I didn't know it was yours,' said Ben helplessly.

'No,' went on the man, who was by now at the door ready to leave, 'and I suppose you didn't know that the others were ours when you hid them.'

'What others? I didn't see any others,' said Ben.

'Maybe, maybe not. But when Lomax comes, you'd better think of a better story than that. He's not a nice understanding man like me.'

With a scraping little laugh he went out and they heard the key turn in the lock behind him.

At first they said nothing. Even though they were locked up in this dirty room and their bodies were sore from the treatment they had received, they still found it hard to believe that this was happening to them. They had simply gone to the beach to tidy Boat. How could they be here, trussed up and at the mercy of some violent strangers who believed things about them that weren't true? It was the sort of story that you read in books or saw on TV, but it didn't really happen, did it? If it was TV, the victims would look around the room and see a skylight big enough to crawl through or a piece of glass to cut through their ropes. Charlie and Ben didn't even try. They sat in silence, feeling afraid and helpless.

'They're bound to let us go when they find out we don't know anything about their things,' said Charlie suddenly.

Ben had never heard his voice sound so small and thin.

'Yes,' he said, hearing the same edge in his own voice.

The silence came back into the room. Neither of them liked it. It allowed them to think horrible thoughts about what the men might be planning.

'Teamwork, that's what we need,' said Ben at last.

'Yes,' said Charlie.

'What do they want?'

'I don't know. They're not interested in us though. It's those packages they're talking about. If you hadn't got that rope caught, we'd never have seen them.'

'My fault, then, is it?'

'That's not what I meant. Just think, though. I'm right. If they could get their packages, they wouldn't want us.'

'But how can we convince them we don't know anything about it?'

'I don't know. We can't.'

Charlie's words showed the danger they were in. For a moment, they both thought about what he'd said. The silence was once again oppressive and they preferred to talk. They talked about everything they could think of. They knew that Ben's mother would eventually miss them and start looking for them. That gave them some comfort, but she would have no idea where to look. They didn't even know where they were themselves.

The more they talked, the more obvious it became that there were only two possibilities. The first was if they could convince the men that they'd made a mistake and that they knew nothing about their packages. They both agreed that this didn't seem very likely to succeed. The second was to get out of the house somehow and nearer to a place where they might be seen and helped. It was impossible for them to escape, so they would have to persuade the men to take them out.

'Why should they do that?' asked Ben when Charlie suggested it.

'I don't know,' said Charlie. 'But they think we know where their stuff is, don't they?'

As he said that, Ben had the beginning of an idea.

'We could lead them to their packages,' he said, half to himself.

'How? We don't know where they are.'

'No. But we could pretend we did and promise to show them the place.'

'What good would that do?'

'I don't know,' said Ben. 'It would get us outside, though. And we could say that the packages were hidden near our cottage. They'd have to take us there then. Maybe if they did we could get away.'

The danger of such an idea made Charlie very doubtful about it. Secretly, in spite of his aching body he still didn't believe that this was really happening. He was here with Ben, the friend he walked home from school with. Soon the mistake would be put right and they would be eating a tin of creamed rice on the seat outside their cottage. As they continued to talk, it pushed the fear a little further away and brought back some normality to them. They began to believe that things could turn out right if they were careful.

An hour must have passed since they were put into the room when they heard the van's engine as it bucked its way up the track. It stopped outside and at once they heard voices. There was a new one. It was loud and angry, worse even than the gravelly one of the man who had brought them up here. Immediately they heard banging below them and then heavy footsteps on the stairs. The door opened and Lomax came into the room.

As soon as they saw him, they knew that they were in trouble. He was much bigger than the other two and the expression on his face was black, tight and twisted. His eyes looked as if they'd crawled out of a nightmare and buried themselves in his skull. He looked at the boys and the venom they saw burning there drove all the planning that they had just been doing from their minds. Once again, they felt only blind, blank terror.

CHAPTER ELEVEN – LOMAX

Lomax stood looking at them for ages. His idea was obviously to drain any resistance from them and make them feel just how powerful he was. The dark grey of his beard seemed to be reflected in the heavy circles around his eyes. Everything about him was massive and, for the first time, the boys sensed that here they were dealing not just with crime, but with evil. When he spoke, his voice was quiet but it slid into their minds like a razor.

'Now then. The packages. Where are they?'

Ben had no idea what to say, but he didn't dare remain silent.

'Honest, we don't know. We told your friends. We haven't seen them. The one you found in our boat was the only one. I promise.'

He tailed off. The man was shaking his head and tutting.

'They told me you were saying that. It's garbage. I don't like garbage so I want you to listen carefully. We saw you lifting our packages. There are none left out at the buoy. That means somebody's taken them. Now who else would it be?'

He stopped. They didn't answer. He didn't expect them to. He lit a cigarette and held the still burning match close to Charlie's face before letting it fall to the ground.

'I'm very busy. I don't have time for mucking around. What I want to know, right now, is where you've put the rest of the stuff.'

The boys realised that they had no option. They would have to pretend that they knew where the packages were. If they continued to tell the truth, they wouldn't be believed, and the man would obviously not only do very nasty things to them, but probably enjoy doing them too. When Ben spoke, it wasn't from bravado or heroism, but sheer panic.

'Don't do anything, please,' he begged.

'So talk,' said Lomax.

'My dad said they must belong to somebody,' said Ben. 'We didn't know what they were. We didn't open them or anything. We pretended it was treasure. Like pirates, you know.'

Charlie looked at him in amazement. Lomax's expression relaxed. His voice was even a little encouraging now.

'Good. Now, where are they?'

'We buried them. Under a rock.'

Lomax became suspicious.

'It must have been a big hole,' he said. 'What did you want to bury them for?'

Ben's mind raced. Charlie came to the rescue.

'He doesn't mean we dug a hole. The rock was one of those overhanging ones. It was eroded underneath. The space there must have been well, three or four cubic metres.'

Luckily, Charlie was the only one in the room who had any idea of how much space three or four cubic metres represented.

'Glaciation,' he added, as much to his own surprise as to that of the man.

'We hid it as a sort of joke. For my mum,' added Ben, who had had time to think. 'We were going to go for a walk with her and pretend to find it. We thought there might be a reward for it. We were going to take it to the police.'

Lomax grabbed his arm roughly.

'Does anybody else know about it?'

'No,' said Ben, squealing with the pain.

'What about the police?' Lomax went on.

'There hasn't been time. My dad hurt his leg. He's had to go to hospital.'

'I don't believe a word of this,' said Lomax, tightening his grip even more.

'Leave him alone. It's true,' shouted Charlie. 'He's in Inverness. It's a fracture of the tibia. Just a simple one. Three days observation, that's what he'll need, they said. When they break bones need ...'

'Shut up,' yelled Lomax. 'I'm not talking about your father. I'm talking about our stuff.'

'He's not my father,' said Charlie, not knowing why he was risking the man's anger, but wanting very much to make him let go of Ben's arm. 'I'm just a friend. I was going to Portugal on holiday in August, but Ben ...'

'I said shut up,' Lomax shouted again, releasing his grip on Ben and raising his hand as if to hit Charlie across the face. Charlie ducked in anticipation. Ben rubbed his arm.

'Mister,' he said. 'We're frightened. We're not making it up. We wouldn't dare.'

'You probably would,' said Lomax. 'I don't trust any kids nowadays. OK, let's prove it then. Where's the stuff hidden?'

'It's difficult to describe the place,' said Ben, thinking fast. 'It's near our house. On the hill behind it.'

'Where?' insisted Lomax.

'Honestly, I don't know how to explain it,' Ben said. 'I know how to get there, but it's not easy to describe because so many of the paths and rocks look alike.'

'OK. There's a simple answer to that. You can take us there.'

Ben looked quickly at Charlie and saw the same flash of hope that he had himself felt at the words. They began to get up. Their hopes crashed as Lomax spoke again.

'Not both of you.'

He pointed at Charlie.

'You stay here.'

'But he knows where it is too,' said Ben. 'I might forget.'

Lomax's face came close to his.

'He stays here,' he said, with iron in his voice. 'Our insurance policy in case you get clever.'

He bundled Ben out of the room, leaving Charlie wide-eyed and whimpering quietly. Their plan had gone badly wrong. For a moment, Ben thought of confessing that they were lying, but he knew very well what Lomax's reaction to that would be. As he was bundled out of the cottage, it was a great surprise to find that he had only one thought in his head; he was determined to get back together with Charlie before the afternoon was over.

He was pushed into the back of the van and Lomax and the driver got into the front. They reversed and turned down the track again onto the road.

'Where do we go then?' asked the driver.

'I don't know,' said Ben. 'I don't even know where we are.'

Lomax hoisted him up and jammed him against the backs of their seats.

'Look then,' he said. 'And don't get smart.'

Ben watched the road very carefully, knowing that he would have to remember it if he did manage to get away so that he could get help back to Charlie. They drove through the village of Laide and it was heart-breaking for Ben to see some men standing talking at the pumps of a filling station there. The thought that he could shout to them for help was immediately crushed as Lomax pushed his head down behind the seats until they were well past them.

All the time that they were driving along, Ben's mind was searching for some way to get free. His excitement grew as they drove down into Aultbea. But as they neared the village, Lomax once again pushed him down into the van out of sight. When he was allowed to look once more his throat tightened painfully and he almost cried out. They were driving along the edge of the loch on the road which led right to their cottage. Ewe Island lay out there, changeless, unaware of his danger, the same tranquil sleeping beast that it had been for centuries. Silently, Ben called to the spirits that lurked on it, but if they answered, he heard nothing and found no hope. Lomax suddenly pushed him down again.

'OK kid, down you go. We don't want Mummy seeing you with the bad man. do we?'

Ben felt every turn of the road, knew when they were passing the track down which Boat still lay on her beach and he ached with the knowledge that the things he loved were so close but still out of reach. When the van stopped, he still hadn't worked out any plan.

'Right,' said the big man, turning round to him. 'You said the hill behind your house. Well, this is it.'

Ben was allowed to look again. The van had stopped at the top of the steep slope that ran down from the peninsula into Mellon Charles. It had followed the road until it petered out. The driver had then turned it to face back the way they had come. Once again, Ben was looking down on Ewe Island. He was desperate to get out.

'Yes. It's not far from here,' he stammered.

'OK' said Lomax. 'Out then. Let's get going.'

As the men came round to let him out, Ben tried to think clearly. He couldn't pretend for much longer. Soon they would know something was wrong. The door opened and he was dragged out. He fell onto the road and a small twinge of pain in his ankle gave him an idea. He screamed.

'I said no smart stuff,' said Lomax.

'No, no,' moaned Ben, still lying on the ground. 'It's my ankle. I think I've twisted it.'

'Very funny,' said Lomax. 'But you'd better try to walk on it or I might just snap it for you.'

It was obvious that he meant it, but Ben knew that a limp would earn him some time, so he got up and immediately screamed then collapsed again. Lomax towered over him.

'Listen, kid. You're too clever for your own good. On your feet and get moving or you'll never see your little mate back there again.'

Once more Ben struggled up and this time took two steps before falling again. The driver was looking round nervously as he had done on the beach.

'Let's get away from the road, Lomax.'

Lomax turned again to look at Ben. He wasn't sure whether he was fooling or not.

'Untie him,' he said to the driver, 'and give him a hand.'

Ben felt that he had won a little victory. The ropes were taken from him and the driver put out his arm for Ben to lean on as they started out onto the peninsula. Thanks to the invented sprain, progress was quite slow. All the time, he was trying to work out how to get away. At first he thought that he would simply choose a convenient spot and run as fast as he could. The problem there was that although he was fitter than the two men, they would both be quicker than he would over a short distance. They also had the van and even if he got away they would know where he was heading. As he staggered on, forcing the driver to stop more and more often and insisting that he could hardly stand because of the pain, the second idea came to him. It began to form when he fell in mock agony and felt the dampness of the ground. It was a much more drastic scheme, but if it worked, it would give him a real chance to get away.

At last he saw what he'd been searching for. The three big round rocks had very distinctive patterns on them caused by the grey and yellow lichen on their surface. He fell deliberately once more and made it seem very difficult to get up again. Still sitting on the ground, he said, 'That's it. Just over there.'

The men looked at the rocks.

'Those three?' asked Lomax.

'No, further on,' said Ben, struggling to his feet and grimacing to show how much it was supposed to be hurting him.

'On your way, then. Let's get to it,' said Lomax eagerly.

He went on towards the three rocks as Ben and the driver struggled painfully along behind him. When he got to them, he stopped and turned to yell back.

'Well, where is it? Which one?'

He was some thirty yards ahead of them. Ben could see the end of the bowl-shaped rock beyond him. He pointed to it.

'There. The big round one. Underneath that,' he shouted and seemed to stumble once more.

As he struggled to get up, the driver was watching Lomax. Ben looked too, and prayed that he wasn't mistaken. Lomax was pressing on towards the rock.

Suddenly his arms waved and he seemed to lean to one side. They heard a shout. Lomax took another step and immediately fell forward. The shout he gave then was no longer one of anger, it had become shrill with alarm. Ben had sent him straight into the marsh that his father had warned them about when they had walked this way last week. At first the ground was simply spongy as it had been for most of the way, then it had begun to move under the big man's feet. He felt the first rush of panic. But by then he was too far into it to escape and his movements were too quick. The whole area seemed to become liquid and suddenly, he had sunk to his hips and still his feet had touched nothing solid. His search for the packages was forgotten. He was terrified. This was a dreadful unknown thing. He was on earth that was empty. He had fallen through liquid ground and felt the thick softness clutching at his legs and drawing him further down into its dark insides. He screamed at the driver to help him. The driver looked at Ben. He still hadn't understood what had happened. He tried to get Ben up, but Ben dragged and staggered. Lomax's screams became even louder.

At last, the driver realised what was going on. He left the still moaning Ben lying on the ground and ran to help Lomax. At once, Ben was on his feet and flying back the way they had come. Both the men were too busy to notice him go and his fear and the thrill of escaping made him run faster than he had ever run before. At first he thought of running all the way to their cottage to shout for his mother, but he had already realised that he would be overtaken before he got there. He still had to save Charlie as well. He would have to stop them using the van. He changed direction and headed up the slope towards the place where it was parked.

The driver stood helplessly at the edge of the marsh looking at the floundering Lomax without knowing what to do. He wasn't going to risk getting stuck himself, but every movement that Lomax made sent him deeper. The driver looked round for something to throw across the surface and saw the planks at the edge of the dangerous patch. He fetched one and let it fall towards Lomax. The first try left it just out of his reach. His struggles to reach it took him lower. The driver pulled the plank back again and this time made so sure that it was far enough in that it actually hit Lomax on the head as it fell. Lomax, whose terror had increased as he had been held by the sucking earth, grabbed gratefully at it and began to haul himself along towards safety. It took a long time because every effort he made seemed to make the marsh grip him that much more greedily. With the help of the driver, though, he at last dragged himself on to firmer ground. His breath grated through his throat, his shoulders heaved, and he sat shaking with shock and still half-paralysed with fear at the fate that he had so narrowly escaped.

Suddenly, the two men realised that Ben had gone.

'He knew what he was doing,' said the still shaking Lomax. 'He sent me in there. He knew what would happen to me.'

He forced himself to stand up on unsteady feet.

'Catch him,' he hissed. 'I want him. Find him and bring him back here. Let's see how he likes it in that marsh. And this time, there won't be anybody nearby with a plank.'

CHAPTER TWELVE – ESCAPE

All this time, poor Charlie had been sitting in his prison with only his imagination to distract him. His arms hurt where the ropes were gripping them and the silence pressed heavily on him like a threat. He could hear no sound in the rest of the house. He had to try to get away. But first, he had to find out if he was alone. He took a deep breath and shouted as loudly as he could. It gave him such a satisfying feeling that he shouted some more and started kicking his heels against the floor. In the stillness the din he made was incredibly loud. Almost immediately he got his answer. He wasn't alone. The footsteps stamping up the stairs told him so.

'What the hell's all that about?' said Gravel-voice angrily as he flung open the door.

Charlie thought fast. The pain of the ropes helped him.

'The ropes,' he said, 'they're hurting.'

'Tough,' said the man.

'No. You don't understand,' said Charlie quickly, afraid that he would go away again. 'It's my blood. I've got … haemoglobula.'

The hesitation before the word showed that he had invented it. The man didn't seem to notice.

'What's that?' he asked suspiciously.

Charlie had no idea. As far as he knew, there was no such thing.

'It's a blood disease,' he said. 'It's very rare. I have to take pills every four hours.'

'Tough,' the man said again.

'That's why I told you about my arms,' Charlie went on. 'I've got to keep my blood going properly. If it slows down at all, I get … myoxis.'

Again the hesitation showed that he was inventing it. He'd almost said myxomatosis, but just remembered in time that that was something to do with rabbits.

'I get convulsions,' he added. 'I could even die. Dr Glebe wrote to my mother about it. He sent a note to school too. He said that the white corpuscles need to be thinned so that the inflammation of tissues wouldn't be …'

'Shut up.' said the man as Charlie got into his stride.

Charlie changed his tone.

'I'm not asking to be let out,' he said weakly. 'I just want my arms untied. I can't get away, can I? You don't want me having convulsions here, do you?'

'Listen kid,' said the man. 'I couldn't care less if you convulsed yourself all over Scotland.' He looked at Charlie for a moment, then said, 'OK, I'll untie you. But if I find that you've been having me on, I'll put them ropes back so tight that they'll meet in the middle.'

Charlie was afraid to say anything else in case the man changed his mind. He sat still, trying to look like someone who had haemoglobula and who was about to get myoxis, while the man reached round behind him and loosened the knots. As he felt the ropes slacken, Charlie wriggled his shoulders gratefully and they fell around his feet.

'Thank you very much,' he said, meaning every word of it.

The man picked up the ropes without a word. He went to the door, stopped and pointed a finger at Charlie.

'Any more trouble and these go back. But this time around your neck. Understand?'

Charlie nodded. The man slammed the door and turned the key in the lock.

Charlie was amazed. It had been so simple. His arms were free and he could move around the room much more easily. The small victory made him feel slightly better. If he could achieve that much, surely he could think of a way of actually getting out of the place altogether. He began to stalk quietly about the room, looking everywhere for some sort of inspiration. Ben was out there somewhere. He must try to join him.

***

The van was just under a mile from the marsh. Ben had got a start on the two men. His first mad dash for freedom had made his lungs burn and his throat hurt, but he had now settled into a steady pace and his breathing was quick and regular. As he ran, he tried to think what he was going to do. He was free, there was no doubt of that. Now he had to get to Charlie. He didn't know if there was a phone in the gravel-voiced man's cottage. The two who had brought him here might be able to contact him from a phone box. The important thing was for him to get to their cottage before they did. That meant finding his mother and driving to Laide. He could see the van now up on the slope but he still didn't know how to stop them using it. He looked back. The men were after him. He needed more time.

Lomax was ahead of the driver. Both of them were suffering. Over the years they had smoked too many cigarettes and their chests were heaving with the strain of this unaccustomed exercise. But Lomax was driven by hatred. He wanted very much to catch Ben, he needed to see him suffer to make up for the fright the boy had given him. No-one got away with doing something like that to Lomax. He forced himself to ignore the rasping of his breath and the protests of his body. He could see the boy in the rocks ahead and they were getting closer to him. Soon they would have him again and they'd take him back to the marsh.

By the time Ben reached the van, Lomax's hatred had spurred him to make up a lot of the ground between them. Ben quickly considered the ideas he had had. Letting down the tyres? No, there was not time for that. Throwing away the keys? They weren't there; the driver must have taken them with him. Pulling some wires out of the engine? He tried to open the bonnet but it wouldn't budge and he didn't know where the release catch was. There was nothing he could do. He looked desperately at the van. Nothing. He banged his hand on the bonnet and gave a long scream of frustration and fear. Lomax heard it and stopped for a moment. He looked at Ben standing beside the van and understood at once that the boy was helpless. His revenge was near. He answered Ben's scream with his own shout. Ben heard it, looked at the mud-soaked figure scrambling up the last part of the slope towards him and felt his veins fill with ice. His mind emptied. His plans all disappeared. In their place surged blind instinct. He must not let himself be caught. Without knowing what he was doing, he opened the van door, got behind the wheel and released the handbrake. The van was on a slope. Immediately, it creaked forward, too slowly at first. Lomax had reached the road. One of the rear wheels bumped over a rock. The van's speed increased. Ben's fingers were wrapped round the steering wheel like bands of hot metal and tears were running down his face.

'Go, go, go,' he screamed at the van.

He heard another voice shouting. It was Lomax. When he saw Ben get into the van he had gathered the little breath he had left to make a final sprint. The shout he gave was one of anger. The van had begun to roll more quickly down the hill away from him. He knew that his bursting lungs and his aching legs would never allow him to catch up with the accelerating vehicle. As the distance between his reaching arms and the van increased, he screeched in fury, stumbled to a halt picked up a rock and flung it after Ben.

Ben was unaware of any of this. He felt the van quicken, fixed his tear-filled eyes on the narrow road ahead, kept on shouting and only slowly began to realise that he had got away.

Unfortunately, there was no time for him to delight in the escape. He had never driven a car before. He had watched his mother and father driving and knew about gear changes and brakes. His father had once shown him all the controls but he'd never had to use any of them. As the van got faster and faster on its bumpy way down the hill, he clung to the wheel and tried not to turn it too violently as it went into the slight bends. He risked looking down and saw the three pedals in the floor. He remembered that the middle one was the brake. He put his foot on it and pushed. The van juddered and he was thrown forward against the steering wheel, hurting his ribs. He had braked too hard. The van had slowed a lot. He let it gather speed again and this time tried braking more gently. It had exactly the effect he wanted. He relaxed just a little, feeling his shoulders drop as some of the tension went out of them. He knew that he could control the van now. It would carry on until they ran out of hill. He concentrated hard on steering and kept his right foot poised just above the brake pedal. For the first time since their capture he began to feel that he was in control of things.

***

Lomax had been joined by the driver. They were both breathing harshly as they leaned forward, their hands on their knees. Lomax was recovering first. He gulped enough breath to give the other man his orders.

'You. After the van. He'll stop at the bottom. Bound to. When you get it, drive over to our place. We'll get the other kid.'

The driver didn't have breath enough to answer. He just nodded.

'I'll go this way,' went on Lomax, pointing across the neck of the peninsula. 'It's not far. I might get there before you. Get going.'

The two men turned to go in opposite directions. Lomax stopped and called.

'If you get your hands on either of them, just keep them. Don't do anything to them. Don't touch them. Save them for me. They're mine.'

He spat on the ground and set off across the peninsula for Laide. The driver wiped the sweat from his forehead and started following the road down which his van had disappeared.

***

The van had rushed straight down the slope and tried to climb the steep hill on the other side, only managing to get a quarter of the way up before it stopped and started rolling back down again. Ben stamped hard on the brake and held his foot down as he pulled the hand brake on. The van was still. Ben's shoulders went limp and his head rested on the steering wheel as he blew out a great sigh of relief. There was no time for relaxation though. The driver still had the keys to the van and if he was following him he could drive it to where Charlie was. He had somehow to get rid of the van. His mind seemed to be racing. He pulled the steering wheel as far round to the right as he could, held on to it and then released the handbrake. The van started to move immediately. Ben jumped clear as it picked up more speed, rolled back across the road and then off the right-hand side. With a tearing sound, it bumped over the edge of the steep bank beside the road, tipped backwards and fell on its side into the soggy ground at the bottom. Ben turned away and started once again to run up the hill towards the cottage.

It was well past lunchtime and his mother was beginning to feel rather anxious about the boys. She was sitting on the seat outside the door when Ben's running figure appeared at the end of the track. She saw him at once and immediately knew that something was wrong.

She ran to meet him and when they met, the way he flung his arms round her and squeezed told her that there was more trouble. Just as he had after his journey from Ewe Island, Ben felt like letting all of his fear come out in tears, but he shook the thought out of his head, took several gulps of air and said to his mother that he would tell her everything that had happened. First, though, she must get into the car and drive over to Laide to get Charlie. His tone was so definite and his mother could so easily see that something awful had happened that she went immediately into the cottage for the car keys and drove off without asking him any questions.

Although Laide was less than three miles away on the other side of the peninsula, the road went back through Aultbea, up over the hill and back down again and it meant a car journey of about six miles. As they drove along the loch and through the village, Ben told the whole story. His mother couldn't believe what she was hearing. Her husband's accident and a break-in had been more than enough to fill their holiday, but tales of kidnapping, threats and imprisonment were ridiculous. Things like this didn't happen. Nevertheless, here they were, driving furiously towards Laide, where poor little Charlie was apparently locked up at the mercy of some criminals.

Neither she nor Ben had any idea what they were going to do when they got there. When she'd phoned the police before leaving, a sergeant had promised that a car would get to Laide as quickly as it could but the problem was that it had to come all the way from Gairloch again. They couldn't count on it arriving in time. It was up to herself and Ben to think up some way of saving Charlie.

***

As they headed north-east along the Laide road, Lomax was still half walking, half jogging due east towards the same point. He didn't know that he would get no help from his driver, who had found his wrecked van and was sitting beside the road trying to get his breath back. But Lomax wasn't thinking of him. He was hurting, his lungs burned, his muscles ached, and all the torments he was having to go through fuelled the hatred in him still further. He wanted to stop. He wanted to sit down and rest until his heart stopped battering away and his body stopped hurting so much. More than all of that, though, he wanted to get his hands on Ben and Charlie so that he could unload all of his own pain onto them. He was more than half way to Laide. It was all downhill from now on.

CHAPTER THIRTEEN – CHARLIE'S PLAN

Charlie had inspected the room carefully but there was nothing that would help him to escape. He thought of breaking the window but it was too small to get through and too high off the ground. He looked at the hinges of the door, but they were concealed, and anyway he had no screwdriver or penknife. There seemed to be only one conclusion. He couldn't use either of the two exits. But the fact that he'd managed to get rid of his ropes had excited him. Everything was possible. And, unlike Ben, he didn't rely on magical interventions by spirits or the other 'dream things' Ben always talked about. That wasn't Charlie's way. He wished he could Google something about escaping, but he couldn't. He'd just have to work things out.

He began to think very carefully through the facts that faced him. He was in a prison. It had only two exits. The window was totally unusable. That left the door. If he was going to escape, it would have to be through that. But it was locked. In books it was easy; somebody found a piece of wire and picked the lock. But there was no wire and he didn't know how to pick locks. In other stories, they battered at the door until it crashed open. Charlie's opinion of himself was quite high, but it was realistic. Any heroics like that would simply give him a sore shoulder and bring the man straight up to carry out some of his threats.

His thinking was simply bringing him round in circles. There seemed to be no solution. Then it suddenly occurred to him that he had missed out the obvious. There was another way of getting out and he'd read about how it was done in one of his books. The realisation brought back all his excitement. He stood up quickly, went to the door and made a thorough examination of it. Yes. It could be done. The only problem was that he needed two particular pieces of equipment and here he was sitting in an empty room.

There was no question now of giving up, though. He knelt on the floor and looked carefully at all the floorboards one by one. When he found what he was looking for, he sat down and began picking at it with his fingernails. It hurt a lot because the wood was old and hard, but he continued to pull up lots of little splinters until he had dug a small piece out of the side of one of the floorboards. When he thought that he had scraped far enough into the edge, he pushed the ends of his fingers into a split in the wood and started to ease it wider. His fingertips were already raw, but he ignored the pain and forced himself to push harder. The piece of wood lifted bit by bit until he heard a small crack and it was free. He clamped his sore fingers under his armpits to ease their hurt and looked triumphantly at the long flat splinter which lay by his knees. It was about eight inches long with a point at one end; the perfect tool for the job he had in mind. He picked it up, carefully tested its strength and placed it on the chair beside the door. The next task was much easier. He took off his jumper, unbuttoned his shirt, took that off too and began, very deliberately, to tear it.

He tore along the two seams at the sides and then across under the neck so that the whole of the back of the shirt came away. When he had finished, he put his jumper and the remains of the shirt back on. In one hand he held the piece of material. With the other he picked up the splinter. He was ready to open the door.

***

As Ben and his mother drove down the hill towards Laide, they still had no idea what they were going to do. They would have to keep the men occupied until the police arrived. The men were stronger and more ruthless than they were, so there could be no question of tackling them face-to-face in any way. Whatever scheme they used would have to rely on tricking the men and getting them away from the house. Maybe then one of them could get in and set Charlie free. At the moment, that was as far as their planning went.

As they approached the signpost telling them that they were entering Laide, Ben suddenly grabbed his mother's arm and shouted, 'Mum. Stop.'

The change in his voice and the urgency of his tone made her do as he said without question. She pulled in to the side of the road.

'What is it Ben?' she asked, turning to him.

He pointed out through the windscreen.

'There look. That's the man. The one with the beard. The one called Lomax.'

Ben's mother looked the way he was pointing and felt at once the horror of the man. He was huge and had the look of a bear as he stumbled down the slope towards the road. Some of the mud from the marsh had dried so that there were patches of grey and black all over him. His beard and hair were matted with filth and sweat, the circles round his eyes were even darker and his powerful hands opened and shut as if he were trying to grab something with them. Even at this distance, she felt the man's evil.

'He's horrible,' she said with a shudder.

'What are we going to do now?' said Ben. 'There's no time to go and get Charlie out, even if we knew how to, and Lomax would get there before we could get away.'

'We'll just have to hope the police come soon.'

'Oh mum, that's no use. Look at him. He's angry. He might do all sorts of things to Charlie. We've got to do something.'

Ben was right, but what could they do? They were no match for a man like Lomax.

'I don't know what,' said Ben's mother, her face screwed up with the worry. 'All he's thinking about is getting back. Whatever I did, he wouldn't take any notice of it.'

Ben was quiet for a moment. He had had an idea. It was obvious, but he hated it.

'He'd take notice of me, though, wouldn't he?'

'What?' said his mother, startled at his words.

'It's me he's mad at, not Charlie,' Ben went on. 'I'm the one he wants. I'm the one who led him into the marsh.'

'Yes, and he can't get you, thank goodness.'

'But he can get Charlie, Mum. And Charlie can't get away. But I can.'

His mother was beginning to see what he meant.

'You can't let him see you,' she said, gripping her son's arm.

'It's the only thing that'll stop him thinking about Charlie, isn't it?' said Ben, hating the words as he said them. 'Anyway, look at him,' he went on. 'He can hardly drag himself along. He's had to run all the way across here. I've had a rest. I can easily keep away from him.'

'No, Ben. You can't do that. I won't let you.'

Her grip tightened on his arm. Ben reached across with his other hand and gently opened her fingers.

'I've got to, Mum,' he said. 'It's the only way. I'll lead him away. You go and get Charlie. I'll meet you at Mellon Udrigle.'

Before his mother could say anything else and before he had time to change his mind, Ben opened his door, got out and jumped across the ditch beside the road. He ran quickly down the hill and hid behind a wall.

His mother was rigid with fear. She couldn't leave her son here with a monster. But already he'd disappeared. He was making his way towards that creature down the road and was going to show himself deliberately to provoke the man. She couldn't allow it. She must make him get back into the car. Where was he? There was no sign of him. She might even be too late. Lomax might already have seen him. The tears were running down her face although she made no sound. She shook her head. Ben had been foolish, but he was doing something. She was just sitting here. The best way she could help him would be to get Charlie right away and then come back with him to fetch Ben. With her head still ringing with the fear at what might happen to Ben, she slammed the car into gear and, on squealing tyres, accelerated down towards Laide. The car flashed past the wall behind which Ben had disappeared, past Lomax who was startled by its sudden rush, and turned to speed through the village towards the house where Charlie was imprisoned.

Behind his wall, Ben was already regretting his decision, but the sound of the car whining away into the distance meant that he must go through with it. He knew that Lomax was tired and he was sure that he could keep ahead of him. But he couldn't just jump out in front of him and yell, 'Catch me if you can'. That would be a bit obvious. No, he would have to pretend that he had come across country too and that he was trying to get to Charlie.

He followed the wall as far as he could. Lomax was still ahead of him. Ben shook himself and prepared for the chase. He moved behind a bank which ran down beside the road into the village and hurried along, keeping his head low until he was sure that he was a long way past Lomax. He stopped, took several deep breaths and whispered, 'You'd better be grateful for this, Charlie.'

Then, without giving himself time to think about it any more, he staggered forward onto the road as if he had just run several miles.

His body was turned away from Lomax, but he glanced back to see the man's reaction. He saw him duck back out of sight and he knew right away that he had been spotted. That was fine. Instead of rushing after Ben straight away, Lomax had hidden himself. He was tired. He didn't want to run if he could avoid it. He'd prefer to creep up on Ben. It was just what Ben had hoped. As long as he pretended not to see Lomax, the man would be in no rush to grab him. It was just a question of staying ahead of him. Ben began to limp along the road, looking very weary.

***

Lomax had recognised Ben immediately. His duck back out of sight had been a reflex action. It gave him time to think. He'd been planning what he would do to the other boy, but here in front of him was the one he really wanted to hurt. But why? How come he was so lucky all off a sudden? What was the boy doing here? How had he got here ahead of him? Lomax didn't trust it. It looked like another of his tricks.

He began to follow Ben, keeping well back into the side of the road. The kid hadn't seen him. Lomax studied him carefully. He did look as if he'd run a long way. He knew his way around. Maybe there was a short-cut. He couldn't have come by road. If he had, his parents must have driven him, so where were they? And where was their car? They wouldn't bring him across here and then leave him alone, knowing what he'd been through already. No, that didn't make sense. He must have come on his own, looking for his friend. Maybe Lomax had got lucky after all. At last. Well, this time, he intended to make the most of it.

In Laide, the main road that runs around Gruinard Bay and on under the shoulders of An Teallach to Dundonnell is joined by another short road. This other road leads out onto the peninsula to a scatter of houses and a cross-roads with directions to nowhere. The place is called Mellon Udrigle. It was this road that Ben took when he reached the point where they meet.

Lomax was surprised and disappointed at first by his choice. He had hoped that Ben would go straight to the house. Gravel-voice could have helped him to catch him then, and they could have dealt with the two kids together. But the boy must have forgotten the way. Then he thought of the wilderness into which he was heading and a tight smile stretched behind his beard. It was a dead end. This time there was no escape. The boy was hurt and tired and he was limping straight into a trap. It was like a lobster crawling down into a creel. Lomax liked lobsters.

***

Meanwhile, Charlie was working on his escape plan. He spread the piece of shirt flat on the floor near the gap at the bottom of the door. Using the sharp end of the splinter he then pushed it bit by bit through the gap until nearly all the material was spread out on the other side of the door underneath the key. The next part of the plan needed lots of luck.

Using the other end of the splinter, he started trying to juggle the key in the lock until it was straight. He had to be careful not to push too hard or the splinter might break and get stuck. The key made slight movements as he pushed, turned and scraped the splinter back and forth inside the lock. At last the key was completely straight in the keyhole. Charlie looked. No light was getting through at all. This was the moment.

With even greater care than before, he pushed the blunt end of the splinter gently against the end of the key. The key moved back in the lock. Charlie was hardly daring to breathe. He pushed a little more. The key slid further. Three more times he gave gentle little pushes and three more times the key moved. On the third there was a click and the key tilted inside the lock. This was it. He inspected the keyhole again, slipped the splinter back in like a surgeon doing an important operation, rested it on the end of the key and gave one more push.

The key gave way immediately. It fell out of the lock and, to Charlie's enormous relief, landed on the piece of shirt. That was the critical moment. If the key had stuck in the lock or if it had fallen onto the floor instead of the cloth, all his efforts would have been wasted. Instead, he had been rewarded. He knelt down and started to pull the piece of shirt back under the door. It came easily and Charlie almost laughed out loud when its precious load came with it. He grabbed the key, kissed it, stood up and got ready for the next step.

His joy was shattered almost immediately. He was slipping the key very gently into the lock when he heard the sound of a car engine. It stopped somewhere back down the path, a car door opened and then slammed shut again. It must mean that the others had come back. All his work was for nothing. His mind raced. He mustn't let them find out that he knew how to get the key in case he could use the same technique again. He decided to open the door and put the key back in the lock outside. He wouldn't be able to lock it of course, but the man might think that he had just forgotten to lock the door when he left.

He turned the key and was soon standing at the open door, pleased that he had managed to get out, but sorry that it would be for such a short time. He jumped back into the room as he heard a knocking downstairs. What could that he? It sounded like the front door. If that was so, it couldn't he the other men and Ben. They would have come straight in. His mood swung back towards hope again. He went out onto the landing and listened. The front door was opened and Charlie nearly called out when he heard the voice of the person who had knocked.

It was Ben's mother, of course. She had driven straight to the house, thinking of Ben back there with Lomax and too worried to work out any sort of plan of action. When she drove up the track, all that she could think of was that somehow she would have to get the man away from the house so that she could get in and let Charlie out. She stopped the car some way down the track, vaguely supposing that she could ask the man to come and look at her engine or something. When he answered the door, she was very nervous. Her voice trembled as she spoke.

'Excuse me. I'm very sorry to trouble you, but I saw your house here and I came up to see if you could help me.'

'What's up?' asked the man, looking past her to see if there was anyone else with her.

His voice startled her and she remembered at once how Ben had described it as scratchy. The thought of Ben calmed her.

'It's my car,' she said, pointing back down the track. 'It seems to be playing up a bit.'

'I don't know anything about cars,' said the man.

'But couldn't you just have a look at it? I'm sure it's something very simple.'

'Even if it was, I still wouldn't know anything about it,' said the man, and he made to shut the door.

Ben's mother thought quickly.

'Yes, but now it's blocking your track here. You won't be able to get up or down. Sorry.'

The man looked at her car. She was right.

'If you can't do anything, perhaps you wouldn't mind giving me a push back onto the road. Just to get it out of your way.'

That made sense to the man. He didn't want garage mechanics nosing around the place, and Lomax would be back soon with the van. The woman's car had to be shifted.

'OK,' he said. 'Come on. I'll give you a shove.'

He walked down the track towards the car. Ben's mother was thinking hard all the time. How could she keep him there? How could she make him wait by the car while she went up to the house? The answer was obvious. She couldn't. He wouldn't let her anywhere near the house with Charlie in there. The man reached her car and stood by the bonnet ready to start pushing it back down the track. Ben's mother's mind was racing and she felt completely helpless. She got into the car, looked at the man thinking that she could perhaps knock him over with the car and hurt him enough to give her time to …

Suddenly, she felt a rush of blood to her face. Behind the man, running from the door of the house, was Charlie. He was heading for some low bushes behind the fence which ran down the left-hand side of the track. She had to keep the man's attention.

'Found it,' she shouted suddenly.

The man jumped.

'What?' he said.

'This,' said Ben's mother. 'Down here look. This was the trouble all along.'

She reached down towards the dashboard in front of her and started the engine. The man came round beside the driver's door and looked in.

'These wires, see? One of them was loose. I can't understand why I didn't see it before.'

She was watching Charlie out of the corner of her eye. He had nearly reached the bushes.

'Typical of me,' she went on, in a silly sing-song voice. 'Always miss the obvious. I'd forget my head if it weren't screwed on. One day my husband told me I ought to write down our address and keep it in my handbag in case I forgot where I lived. I did, and d'you know what? I lost the handbag.'

She finished with a shrill giggle, partly because it suited the character she was pretending to be and partly because she was delighted to see Charlie vanish into the bushes.

'I'll be off now then,' she said. 'Sorry to have troubled you. You've been very kind. Thank you so much. Just one more thing. D'you mind if I drive up to your house and turn around there? This track's a bit narrow.'

'Help yourself,' said the man, anxious to get rid of this talkative idiot.

She drove slowly towards the house, passing the bushes where Charlie was hiding. The man walked back to the house. She took her time turning the car. He waited at the door. She waved to him and he raised his hand briefly as she started down the track again. She looked in her rear-view mirror. The man had gone into the house. She accelerated to where the bushes were. As she came up to them, Charlie appeared immediately. She leaned across, pushed open the passenger door and he scrambled in. The car had hardly stopped and she was sure that the man wouldn't have noticed anything.

Charlie sat back in his seat. His face was white and strained. He reached out his right hand and squeezed her arm. She knew that he would like to have hugged her as Ben had done.

'How are you, Charlie?' she said.

'Fine,' he said, and the unwelcome but very necessary tears began to dribble down his cheeks.

'Just one thing left to do now,' she said to take his mind off what he'd been through.

He looked at her. He wasn't ready yet to risk trying to speak.

'Just got to get Ben,' she said. 'He's waiting for us at Mellon Udrigle.'

As she smiled to convince Charlie that it really was as simple as that, she was hoping and praying that she was right.

CHAPTER FOURTEEN – THE END OF THE CHASE

Ben had been staying a comfortable distance in front of Lomax all the way along the road. He had never looked directly at the man and Lomax still thought that Ben didn't know he was being followed. They had gone about a mile when his patience ran out. He knew that there was no escape. It was time to close for the kill. He moved into the centre of the road.

'OK kid,' he shouted. 'This is it.'

Ben spun round. The sudden shout had startled him. His fear of Lomax jumped in his mind again.

'Surprise, surprise,' said Lomax, moving towards him. 'Thought you'd got away, didn't you? Thought you'd come and get your pal. Well, I've got news for you. You've come the wrong way. That's a dead-end.'

Ben didn't waste any breath answering him. They had stopped at the very foot of Meallan Udrigill. He turned, leaped across the ditch at the side of the road and began scampering up the hill.

It was Lomax's turn to be taken completely by surprise. The weary boy who had been limping painfully along the road was suddenly scurrying away like a rabbit. Already he was well above the road. Lomax saw that he would never catch him now. He'd been fooled again. He swore at the figure as it climbed amongst some rocks on the hillside. But his words froze as he heard a cry and saw the figure fall. He waited. The boy didn't reappear. He saw an arm waving briefly from behind one of the rocks. Yes. It was the boy's arm. The blue and white pattern of his jumper was clear. His luck had turned. The kid had fallen properly this time. He was lying there in the rocks. There was justice in the world after all.

He began the painful climb up the slope to where Ben had disappeared. It was hard work. Lomax had run and walked further today than he normally walked in a week at home, and he wasn't used to these places. Flat city pavements were his usual surfaces, not this springy, spongy turf, these rocks and these endless hills. He ached everywhere but the need to hurt Ben gave him the strength to force his body up towards the rocks where the arm still waved feebly. The nearest rock overhung the slope a little and as he approached it, he could reach up and pull himself around it. The boy's arm stuck out from behind the rock immediately in front of him.

'Right, kid. End of story,' he panted as he staggered forward. He looked down, lifted his head and made the most blood-curdling noise it was possible for any human throat to produce.

Charlie and Ben's mother were just turning off the main road onto the one up which Ben had been leading Lomax. As they drove along, they looked anxiously all around them, Ben's mother concentrating hard on the road ahead and Charlie scouring the slopes on either side. It was as they came by the base of Meallan Udrigill that Charlie shouted, 'Stop. Up there, look. I thought I saw something.'

She stopped the car. They both got out and looked hard.

'Yes. There, look,' said Charlie, pointing at some rocks.

As he spoke, Ben's mother saw it too. Her blood froze. It was Lomax. He was standing among the rocks holding a long stick-like object. It might have been the branch of a tree or the stake from a garden fence. From this distance it was difficult to tell. He lifted it over his head and swung it down viciously at something lying on the ground in front of him. Ben's mother screamed. Lomax heard the sound and looked down at them. He had never seen Ben's mother, but Charlie looked familiar to him. There couldn't be many more kids around here at this time of year, and Lomax wanted blood. He began to run down the slope towards them, out of control, falling and cursing.

Charlie and Ben's mother didn't wait for him. They leapt into the car and drove off up the road towards Mellon Udrigle. They didn't care for the moment that it was a dead end; while they were in the car, they were safe. He couldn't get at them there.

Charlie looked back as they drove along. Lomax was screaming and waving the stick, scrambling down across the rocks on the slope. His anger was driving him hard once again. At the bottom of the hill, he came to the ditch and jumped. When Ben had done it, he'd been sure-footed and knew where to land, but Lomax was clumsy. His foot came down on some loose rocks, which immediately slid from under him, making him roll down to the bottom of the ditch, where a little stream was waiting for him. As he tumbled, he felt his ankle twist and a pain shoot up into his leg. He tried to stand again, but the ankle was too badly twisted. It wouldn't take his weight. With another scream of anger and frustration, he fell back against the side of the ditch. Only his head and shoulders were visible from the road.

Charlie saw it all.

'It's alright,' he said. 'He's stopped. I don't think he'll come after us.'

Ben's mother slowed down and stopped in the middle of the road. She was shaking, her lips were quivering and her face was tight and pale.

'What was he hitting at, Charlie?' she said in the tiniest of voices.

Charlie shook his head. He didn't want to believe what his eyes had told him – that the thing on the ground that Lomax was hitting was Ben. Neither of them knew what to do. They were afraid to leave the car until they were sure Lomax couldn't get up and come after them again. For all they knew, he might be trying to fool them.

'The police will be here soon,' said Ben's mother, and Charlie saw the tears on her face.

The presence of Lomax terrified them. They sat for ages, saying nothing, both of them weary from the events of the past two days, neither of them feeling strong enough to do anything. The evening was beginning to roll its softness down off the hills. Its quiet closed round them.

Then, the stillness was suddenly parted by a voice. It was close by and made them both twitch into immediate, frightened action.

'Can I get in?' it said.

Ben's mother's eyes were wide and wild.

'Ben?' she said. pushing open her door. 'Ben?'

Her son had seen the car from the rocks behind which he had been hiding and made his way down the slope to them, staying out of sight all the way. Now, he jumped out of the ditch beside the road and ran over to her. She clutched him, kissed him, wept, laughed, talked, laughed again, and suddenly remembered Lomax. They both looked down the road.

He was still sitting in the ditch. He had seen Ben's arrival, seen the embraces and even heard their voices, but he couldn't move. When he had got to the rocks and found the empty jumper there, with sticks poked through it to make it stand up and with its arm blowing in the breeze, he had for a moment gone completely mad. Too many things had gone wrong. It was the final deception. The rage into which he fell was genuine madness. He'd picked up the branch and thrashed at the jumper as if Ben were still inside it. The scream he'd heard from Ben's mother made him make his final lunge towards people. He wanted to destroy. It wasn't enough to be beating at the ground or at the boy's jumper, he wanted more. But the effort of running down the slope and the final fall had finished him completely. When they drove easily away out of his reach, his madness was still with him but he could do nothing to satisfy it.

Charlie, Ben and Ben's mother couldn't understand why he hadn't made any move. It was Ben who suggested that they should drive home, saying that Lomax couldn't do anything to them as they drove past him in a car. His remarks made sense. His mother started the engine, drove to a wider section of road in which she could turn and headed back towards Laide. Despite herself, she accelerated fiercely when they approached the place where Lomax was still lying. As they tore by, he shook his fist at them and screamed. If he could have got his hands on them, he'd have … There was no point thinking about it. They'd won.

On the way back towards Aultbea. they saw the police car racing towards them. Ben's mother flashed her lights at it and waved her arm out of the side of the car. The other car pulled up beside her. She told them who she was and explained where they would find Lomax and the cottage. Ben reminded them of the van he had crashed and said that its driver would probably be somewhere near it. The police thanked them, suggested that they should go on home and said that they would call later that evening when they had tidied everything up. Ben's mother drove the rest of the way very slowly and with a feeling of enormous relief that at last the evil influences that had turned their holiday into such a nightmare were being taken away so that they could do them no more harm.

By the time the police did come they had learned the whole story. They said that they'd found Lomax still lying where they'd left him. His ankle was so badly sprained that he couldn't walk. He was his usual nasty self but he hadn't been able to resist and they'd arrested him. Gravel-voice had tried to run away as the car drove up the track to the house, but he was quickly caught. They'd found the van and towed it back onto the road and into Aultbea. Inside it, they found the orange package locked inside a box. It contained drugs that would have been worth thousands of pounds if they'd been sold on the streets.

The driver told them everything. Lomax had arranged it all. The drugs had come from Afghanistan, through Turkey and Holland, and he had decided to bring them ashore in a place where he thought it was easier to avoid the Customs men. He had reckoned that no-one took much notice of small boats going in and out of the more northerly Scottish lochs, so he had arranged for the Dutchman to drop them in Loch Ewe. It was the simplest of plans and if Boat hadn't decided to plough through their mooring line, it might have worked.

Secretly, though, as Ben listened, he suspected that, if he hadn't stopped the men, someone or something else would have. That afternoon, when he'd arranged the jumper so that it would draw Lomax up the hill to him, he'd hidden himself and watched the man climb to the rocks. Lomax's movements were wrong. He didn't know how to walk up that hill. He was completely out of place there among Ben's spirits, earth-priests and myths. And as Lomax had been clubbing the piece of wood angrily at his jumper, Ben had noticed that beyond him out in the bay sat Gruinard Island with its own scars which other men had made on it. Evil came in lots of forms. For the moment, Lomax and his drugs were the nearest. But the Highlands would go on resisting the scourges, whatever shape they took.

Later on, when Charlie and Ben were in bed, they talked on and on about the things that had happened to them. They ached with tiredness, but the joy at being safe and the remains of their excitement kept them turning over all the details of their separate experiences. It was just as Ben was on the very edge of sleeping that some drowsy mumbled words from Charlie made him smile happily into his pillow.

'I set myself a mission today Ben,' he said.

'Oh?'

'Yes. When they took you away from that cottage. The mission was to get back with you before the end of the day.'

'I set myself the same one,' said Ben, feeling very close to his friend.

'Yes. I thought you would,' said Charlie.

'We had lots of help, Charlie,' Ben said after a pause.

'Mmmm,' said Charlie, already dropping further down through the warm velvet of his drowsiness.

'The wind and tide sent that package to us,' Ben mumbled, his words barely audible. 'And the swamp held Lomax for me while I ran away. And the stones made him twist his ankle.'

There were other things too that made Ben sure that the spirits of the mountains had been with them all the time, but he chuckled quietly as Charlie, who wanted to go to sleep, said, 'Yes, but I was the one who unlocked the door.'

***

The holiday was over. They were ready to go home and Ben's father was also ready to be fetched from the hospital in Inverness. The last two days had been spent in total laziness. They had had one short trip in Boat, but they were not entirely sorry when the time came to take down the mast, wrap up the sails, pack all their cases and load up the car.

Ben's mother decided that they would go back along a different road so that they could see even more of this place which had affected them all so deeply. They headed first of all for Poolewe and Ben was delighted to be able to look down onto the loch for the first time and see the whole of Ewe Island stretched along its centre. He and Charlie pointed out the various landmarks – or seamarks – of their voyages and they talked of tacking and reaching, of big winds and of mackerel which were caught but never eaten.

They drove through Poolewe, over its bridge and on across to Gairloch. After that, they left the coast and wound along the road that snakes beside Loch Maree. All the way along, the huge body of the mountain called Slioch reared its peaks over them from the other side. Whenever they looked up, it was there, spread massively along the north-eastern bank.

Ben's mother stopped the car in a big lay-by after a long, winding stretch of road had taken them up out of Glen Maree. It was obvious right away why the lay-by was there. The view back down Loch Maree, past Flowerdale Forest and on to Loch Ewe itself was breathtaking. The three of them stood there, memories of the past two weeks washing back into their minds.

'Beautiful,' said Ben's mother at last. 'And it's been here for thousands of years.'

Ben just nodded. Charlie just stood. The silence billowed between them. Grasses blew. The rows of mountains backed away into a blue distance. Ben knew that he and Charlie were going back to a world where everything was smaller and sort of temporary. Back there his inventions would be stronger now because he had lived for a while in a kingdom of mysterious spirits, feeling that the forces he had always sensed straining in earth and trees were real and worth more than the accidental things that they heard on the news.

Eventually, it was time to drag themselves away.

'Come on boys,' said Ben's mother. 'Into the car.'

'Yes,' said Ben. 'It'll still be here when we come back. It'll never change, will it?'

'No,' said his mother confidently.

'I'm glad,' said Ben. 'It's good that some things never change.'

Charlie was still transfixed, looking down at the rows of peaks which seemed to be trying to see past one another as they peered over each other's shoulders.

'Everything alright Charlie,' asked Ben's mother.

'Yes,' said Charlie, shrugging himself out of his dream. 'I was just trying to work out the average height of those peaks. It must be …'

He didn't finish his sentence. Two pairs of arms grabbed him, a hand was clapped over his mouth, and he was carried to the car and pushed into the back seat.

'You're right Ben,' said his mother, as she strapped herself in and started the car. 'Some things never change.'

As they drove away from where the mountain spirits live, the car was full of laughter.